Copyright © 2019 by Hector Platt

All rights reserved. This book or any portion thereof may not be reproduced or used in any manner whatsoever without the express written permission of the publisher except for the use of brief quotations in a book review.

ISBN: 9781076004888
Imprint: Independently published

Contents

The First 5

Soul 9

Sweet Revenge 13

We Are Here 17

The Quiet One 21

Into The Night 26

Swim 32

Stranger 36

Caller 40

Hunger 44

Darkness 49

Can You Keep A Secret? 55

In the Mirror 60

The Morgue 65

Truth or Dare 69

Three Wishes 73

Killer Mask 77

Prisoner 83

Basement 87

His Pet 91

Smile 95

Granny 100

Sally 104

Captured 108

Hiding	112
Carnival	117
Fortuneteller	122
Dare You	127
It's Not Real	132
What Happened to Jamie?	137
SAMANTHA	142
Whistling Train	147
They Always Come Back	152
The Curse.	157
Shadow	162

Description.

Don't you know it's not safe to go out at night? Don't you know it's not safe to be alone when the moon is so bright? Into the woods where everything is silent. So far away that no one can hear you scream.

The First.

It was dark, the sky was clear that night. The stars were shining brightly. She could smell the rain from earlier in the evening.
She came out into the woods when she liked being alone. It was quiet and peaceful, and she had time to think.
Walking through the woods, stepping on thin tree branches, and hearing them crackle under her feet, she smiled.
That's when she heard heavier footsteps. She stopped. Listened and looked around. The moon was high in the sky, so she didn't need the flashlight that she'd been carrying.
There was silence. Nothing, as she continued to listen for maybe a woodland creature.
"You're hearing things." She muttered to herself, shaking her head as she continued to walk.
The more she walked, the more she heard the heavy footsteps. It sounded like they were right behind her. She continued walking, looked over her shoulder, nothing was there.
"Stop doing this to yourself." She glared; how could she be so spooked? She was never like this.
Then again, she never had to worry about someone being out there.
She walked faster, her heart racing.
A few more steps she would be in the clear. The field, and she could run for miles, she was a fast runner.
If someone was behind her, she could outrun them. She knew she could.

That's when her foot gave out, slipping in the mud so that she landed on her back.
The mud created from the rain earlier.
She screamed when she hit her head off the rock that was embedded in the ground.
That's when she saw him.
She knew that she hadn't been hearing things.
The man stood over her, he didn't talk to her.
In his hooded mask he stared at her through the holes of where his eyes were. A white mask with a smile etched into it.
"Don't hurt me!" She cried out.
Her voice echoed through the woods, but no one could hear her. She was miles away from town.
"You will be my first." He grunted.
The voice didn't even sound human. It was creepy and she didn't know what he meant by it.
"Just let me go, please." She whispered.
Her voice sounded strange to her own ears.
Begging and pleading for him to just let her be, act as if he hadn't bumped into her.
"You will be my first of many." The voice came back.
That's when she saw that he was raising his arms over his head, in his hands he held an axe. A brand-new shiny axe.
She could see it glimmer in the moonlight.
"NO!" She screamed, closing her eyes tightly.
If he was going to kill her, she couldn't watch.
Opening her eyes, she saw the blade of the axe just inches from her throat.
He had stopped.
Who was he? She didn't know.

He was playing games with her.

He did it a few times, each time she screamed louder and louder. Not knowing if it was going to be the first time.

"I love the sound of fear. I love the smell of it." The man laughed at her.

This time he brought the axe all the way down, this time she didn't close her eyes like all the times before.

She didn't think that he'd really do it.

He watched as her head rolled down the rest of the way to the edge of the field and he chased it.

Picking her head up by the hair, watching the fresh blood drip, he put it in the sack that he'd brought with him.

This would be the first of many to add to his collection.

He was a collector of many things.

Walking across the field he went to his car and got in, putting her head in the passenger side seat he smiled at her.

"You should consider yourself privileged. You were the first of many. The first beautiful trophy that I will hang on my wall." He kept the mask on as he drove away from the field.

He drove further and further out of town.

They would soon realize that it wasn't safe. It was never safe in the woods. It was never safe being alone.

The End

Description

They come in but they never leave. They aren't allowed to. The new ones don't know what the asylum can do to them. Sally is about to find out that she will never be the same again.

Soul

She'd been there a while. Locked up in this insane asylum. The only one dressed as a clown, the only one that didn't talk. She stared out the window all the time. Rain or shine until it was time to go to bed. She was always looking. Always looking for someone new and it never happened.
Not until that day.
The painted-on smile she wore, never matched with her own. She felt it creeping across her face when she saw the girl with scraggly blonde hair, a dirty face and a blanket she was covered with; a blanket when she walked into the asylum.
Soul walked out of the game room. She walked down the hall to get a better look. The girl looked at her but didn't smile.
It had been a long time since Soul had seen a new one.
Soul slowly walked up to her, wearing her orange clown wig.
"My name's Sally." The girl introduced herself, her voice was low, almost to where Soul couldn't hear her.
"Soul." She responded, licking her lips and seeing just how fragile Sally was.
She had been signed in.
It didn't matter how long Sally was going to stay. Soul would have what she wanted that evening.
Everyone asked her why she called herself Soul.
Sally was no different. She had asked and just like all the other times Soul didn't tell her.

She would find out soon enough.
Sally watched how strange she acted, watched as Soul continued to stare at her most of the day until it got dark.
Just before bed Soul was at her own window. The door opened.
"Don't you sleep?" Sally asked, coming into the room that they now shared.
"Come." Soul whispered, pressing her face against the window.
Sally walked over to her slowly.
Outside in the parking lot it was raining. The thunder was booming, lightning sparked across the sky.
Sally saw another clown, then another, and another. She had lost count.
"Why are they here?" Sally's eyes grew wide.
Soul didn't say anything as she took Sally's hand and opened the bedroom window.
"You're crazy, I'm not going out there." Sally shook her head, tried to pull away.
Soul was stronger than she was.
She pushed Sally out the window and went out after her.
Sally tried to scream, she opened her mouth, no sounds came out.
Soul wasn't fazed, she knew she was crazy. It was the reason she was here.
Soul brought her across the parking lot.
"What are you doing?" Sally tried to be louder, but her voice was as quiet as a squeaking mouse.
Soul knew not to answer her.
She would find out. Just like the rest of them had.
"You brought fresh meat." The tallest clown smiled.

Soul nodded her head.
He took Sally by the shoulders roughly.
Soul had a smile on her face, it was almost time!
She had been waiting for this for so long now.
"They never leave." Soul whispered in Sally's ear.
Sally shivered as the words crept into her head.
The words echoed, the only words that she would hear in her head the rest of the time that she was there.
Forever.
'They Never Leave.'
Sally opened her mouth to scream and Soul brought her mouth just inches from her, sucking the air out of her.
The clowns cheered and clapped, they jumped from one foot to another doing a small jig.
Sally was different when Soul pulled away from her.
"I collect souls." Soul whispered against Sally's ear.
Sally's eyes were dark and distant. She nodded her head and with no resistance she allowed Soul to take her hand leading her back to the window that she had been pushed out of just minutes ago.
Soul licked her lips.
That was the sweetest soul she'd ever taken. Getting into bed Soul couldn't keep the smile off her face.

Description.

Revenge is sweet when you do it right. When it's planned out. He had everything planned out for all that they'd done to him. How could they treat him like that and think they could get away with it? They weren't going to, none of them were. He was going to

show them; he hadn't forgotten what they'd done.
The way they had burned him, how could he forget?

Sweet Revenge

He had her, there was no point in hiding his face. No one was going to hear her scream, no one was going to see her again.
There she was beside the fire that he had created outback. Her hands tied behind her. She was screaming as loud as she could.
"No one can hear you. You're getting what you deserve. Look what you've done to me!" He shouted, pointing at his face reminding her of what she'd done.
"No, it wasn't my fault." She cried shaking her head. She felt the tears sliding down her face. She knew that it wasn't her fault.
"Let me take you back to that night." He grunted.

He was standing there in front of the girls. They told him they were going to play a little game of fire and ice. So, he played. They said it was going to be fun, that he would be popular at school the next day. He trusted them.
They had him close his eyes. He had to keep them shut, if caught he would be out of the game. The last thing he wanted was to be the loser that he was, thinking this game would change him.
He shut them tightly and that's when he felt the burning across his face, the burning on his cheeks, his nose and that's when he opened his eyes. The burning went inside.
They were rubbing the coals from the fire all over his face, they were laughing!

"Look at him, scary scarred boy!" They laughed and danced around him while he screamed louder and louder.
They didn't throw water on him until they saw his flesh burning off. They soaked him buckets of ice water, making the burns hurt more across his face. They left him there when they were done. Left him there to rot. His vision blurred; he knew he was crying but he couldn't feel them running down his face. He couldn't feel anything on his face but the burning sensation.

"I feel it all the time. Now you're going to feel the same thing I do. You're going to feel what I have had to feel!" He shouted at her.
She shook her head back and forth, closed her eyes tightly, she couldn't look like him, it had been long ago what had happened to him, they were just kids.
"Only you're going to keep your eyes open." He whispered against her ear.
He waited until the coals were nice and hot. Embers that would ignite another fire, but that's not what he was going to do.
He took a thick work glove, one that fire couldn't burn through. He picked the embers out of the pit. Showing no mercy, he kept one of her eyes open with one hand.
He rubbed the coals all over her face, her screams were music to his ears. He didn't feel any remorse as he continued to slide it.
The more she cried and screamed the harder he pressed the coals against her face. Then at the last

second right into her eye before getting the ice-cold bucket of water.

He splashed it on her face and then walked away.

"You did this to yourself. You are the one who made this happen." He told her and walked into the house. He would sleep sound tonight. Hearing the painful screams from a distance. The same screams that once came from his own mouth.

There was no use in helping her. They never helped him. She was scarred for life. Just as he had been.

He was going to make her feel just as miserable as he did every day for the rest of her life.

The smile grew wider across his face.

"Sweet revenge." He whispered to himself as he climbed the stairs and went into his bedroom. Getting under the sheet he could hear her painful screams growing louder and louder.

The End

Description.

She wanted the perfect house, one that could tell a story. She picked the oldest one. No neighbors, just her with her thoughts. She thought it was grand, the way the old house stood. Old houses like this one told stories. Stories of spooky tales, ones that would haunt dreams. She didn't realize just how this house was going to change her life. She didn't realize just how life-changing it was going to be.

We Are Here

"We are here." The whispers surrounded her.
They weren't soothing as she tossed from side to side in her bed. She knew that it was an old house, old houses normally told amazing stories.
Those were the words that whispered to her in her dreams, whispered to her through the day and how painful they sounded.
"Who's there?" She asked, sitting up in bed.
The bedroom was dark, there were no streetlights. No neighbors that she could go to.
The voices stopped.
Nothing but silence.
"I heard you. What are you doing here? Who are you?" She asked again, getting ready to climb out of bed.
Her vase on the shelf flew across the room, smashing against the wall.
"What do you want from me?!" She cried out, her heart hammering against her chest.
No one had warned her about the voices. Cries of past memories, she was sure of it.
"Get out, get out of this house while you still can."
Her ears had heard.
It was a man's voice.
A warning, threatening but a warning none the less.
"I'm not leaving. There's no reason to." She called back, letting the voice know that she couldn't be scared that easily.

Swords on the walls were clanging. Swords had been there before she even entered the home. It was her first time seeing them earlier that evening.

"You can't scare me!" She shouted, this time putting her feet on the floor.

She felt a cool draft at her ankles. The draft tugged and tugged until she started screaming. Her voice growing louder and louder.

"Leave before it's too late." The voice whispered in her ear.

She was sweating. Running a hand through her dark black hair. Her eyes wide as she tried looking for a shadow.

The tugging stopped and she ran from the room, slamming the door behind her.

She ran into the bathroom, turning on the light.

When she looked in the mirror a girl was standing in the tub.

"We are here." The girl whispered.

Her black, scraggly, hair over her face, her black eyes looked up at her and she ran from the bathroom.

What had happened in this house? Who was trying to scare her away?

She ran down the stairs, almost missing a step.

"Please leave me alone!" She shouted, pulling at the doorknob, she tried turning and twisting it, but it wouldn't open.

Why wouldn't the door open!?

She heard the whispers behind her.

"We are here, we are here." It repeated like a song over and over again.

"Let me out!" She hollered, her hands sweating as she tried to pull the door open.

"Time has run out. We are here and so are you." The whispered voices surrounded her, coming in closer and closer.

That's when it dawned on her, she had heard about this house.

Before she saw that it was up for sale.

The house was what kept them trapped. The spirits in the house were prisoners and there was nowhere to go.

The house had claimed another victim.

Her as the victim.

"Join us, there is no escape." The voices sang round and round in her head.

A song that would never stop.

The screams were hers now and hers alone. The door would never open again. Never would she see the light of day.

Forever she would be a screaming spirit until the next victim came along.

A new victim that would try and warn, but just like herself they would think it was crazy. They wouldn't heed the warning. It would always be too late, no matter how hard she tried.

It would always be too late to leave.

The End

Description.

Memories haunted her; it was as if it had only happened yesterday. Day in and day out she waited by the window in hopes that he would come. In hopes that he would forgive her for the mistake that no one should ever make. Everyone thought she was crazy, but that's what happens when you lose your one and only child. Thinking that you hear them, thinking that you see them. Spirits from the beyond that tell a story. No one comes to see her, what had happened was an accident. One that she had even created herself. There was no justice for what had happened, unless you call what takes place justice. You can decide for yourself…

The Quiet One

How strange it was, a woman who never left her room; she stared out the window to the backyard pond. Always her eyes were trained there.
A woman of twenty-three with pale skin, light blue eyes, brown hair that was graying already from the stress that she carried. The pain that was deep inside of her.
The pond, it was always the pond that brought her to the window as if she was going to see him, there had been a few times where she had thought she'd seen him.
Blooded and trying to get out of the pond.
A little boy. Her little boy.
She had been sleeping. The nanny was supposed to be watching him. She knew the pond was where alligators swam. A swampy pond and yet she was nowhere to be found.
She had woken up to her son crying and screaming for help.
Rushing to the window she saw him, trying to dig his way out. Trying to claw his way out of the pond.
When she rushed down to save him, he had one leg, one arm, and one eye. She cradled him; help couldn't come fast enough.
She watched the window, hoping to see her little boy again.
Hoping that he would forgive her so that she could forgive herself.

She didn't care about eating, didn't care about talking to anyone. No one came by anymore. She wouldn't answer the door.

No one blamed her, she knew that. The nanny, she got away with it. It was an accident. That's what they called it.

She felt the tear slowly roll down her face.

The alligators had moved on long ago.

A new sound, scratching on the door.

A small smile came across her face.

She had been waiting a long time to hear it.

The scratching noise grew louder and louder a little at a time.

"I know it's you." She whispered, the first and only time taking her eyes away from the window. Away from the pond.

"Come in." Her loving voice responded.

The doorknob jiggled a little.

How she wanted to go and open it.

She knew who was there.

It had to be done on its own.

"Open the door. Come and see me." Her voice was gentle. So soft and so sweet.

The door finally opened it, opened a little more almost as if slow motion.

"There's no need to be afraid now." She encouraged who had opened the door.

She walked towards the door like she was in a trance. No one would be able to save her, no one was there to save her. To look after her. She had pushed them all away knowing this day would come. Knowing she wasn't crazy like they had all thought she was.

Her little boy.

One leg, one arm, just one eye and a smile on his face.
She could see that he had no teeth, his wet flesh was falling off the more he walked into the room.
"Mommy." His little boy voice sounded.
It was like music to her ears. She loved the little boy, it didn't matter how he looked, it was her little boy. She got on her knees, welcomed him into her arms and held him so tightly the smell of him wanted to make her puke but the smile on her face was the best she'd had since he had gone away.
"Come with us Mommy, come and play in the pond." The little boy struggled out from her arms and took her by her hand.
She got up and let him lead her out of the house, slowly they made their way to the pond.
"There is nothing here. They are all gone." She whispered, feeling the sadness taking her again as it always had in the past.
"Come with us mommy. They want to see you." He continued leading her into the pond.
As soon as her foot touched the water, he pulled her under, wrapping her in a death roll. She struggled. She tried so hard to get away.
The harder she struggled the tighter the death roll became.
He had become the alligator in human form. He had become the last survivor and as her eyes began to lose life, she could see them all now.
They were swimming towards her. They all looked like her little boy. That's where she had found peace. This is where she belonged.

"You will forever be able to play now mommy." The little boy's voice whispered in her ear.

The loving sound of her son.

She knew he'd come.

She knew she had seen him before, and this was proof that she had.

The house wasn't her home, the loneliness wasn't her home. Where she belonged was with her son.

Little did she know dead or alive he was going to make her suffer over and over again as he had once suffered while he was alive.

The sweet smiles turned to horrible screams, but sweet to his ears. Justice had been served. Now there was only one more to get. One more to find.

The nanny...

His job wasn't finished, his spirit not being able to rest until he got exactly what he deserved beyond the pond that had taken him...

The End

Description.

A crime of passion is what he called it, justifying what she'd done to him. How could she hurt him like that? How could she take his feelings and tear them out as if he had none? He would get his revenge on her. She would know what it felt like to have her heart bleed in the palm of his hand. The passion and anger that was running through him. He had only meant to scare her, nothing more. It had gone too far but he was happy, happy until the tables turned on him.

Into The Night

Like a ghost he slipped in and out so easily. He laughed at himself as he thought about how easy it was to get away with murder.

She had it coming though, the way she taunted him, the way she teased him. He had lost control thinking he would only go see her and confront her.

She had played him.

Going over to her house to spend movie night together. She didn't know that he was coming over. It was more like a surprise knowing that she was sad.

He didn't know that she had a boyfriend though. It crushed him to see her in his arms. The way she laughed, the way she smiled at him.

The same way that she had smiled when he was with her. How could she give her boyfriend the same smile?

Walking through the door he watched her, watched them until he got up and left. Hiding in the closet off the kitchen.

It was then and only then that he'd shown himself. After her boyfriend had left her. Telling her he loved her was more than he could stand. The self-control he had was like no other.

She screamed when he popped out of the closet. No one could hear her. Being home alone, her boyfriend long gone.

"You don't know what you've done." He growled at her.

She tried running, how she tried running to get out of the house.

He was much faster than she was.
Slamming it shut and locking the door.
He played cat and mouse with her for a short time until she tried hiding down in the basement. She was trapped.
"There's nowhere to run, nowhere to hide." He laughed slowly coming down the stairs after her, locking the door behind them.
"How long did you think that you were going to be able to play this game?" He asked, his anger growing.
She whimpered in the corner she had tucked herself away behind some boxes in hopes that he wouldn't find her.
He laughed as he got closer and closer, looking over the boxes he could see her shaking. Her face pale, the smile that she had on earlier was nowhere to be seen.
Picking her up by the head of her hair she screamed in pain.
She followed him to the workbench. She didn't have a choice.
She was gasping and crying, the tears soaking her face.
"You shouldn't have treated me like I was the only one." He hissed in her ear.
He took the ice pick off the bench and stabbed her with it, the lights flickered in the basement. He covered her mouth to silence the screams.
"No one is going to hear you. No one is going to find you." He growled low against her ear as he drove the ice pick deeper and deeper.
He didn't stop until the handle was pressed against her chest, the blood seeping out with every flicker of the lights in the basement.

He didn't stop until he felt her go limp in his arms.
How heavy she was when she was relaxed.
When she was dead.
"I thought that you were a nice girl. I thought you were someone that I could go to, someone that would love me." His hands were shaking as he let her body drop to the floor.
The lights continued to flicker as he carried her body and brought her outside to the car. He made sure that no one was watching, there were no witnesses.
Putting her in the backseat he was smiling now as he drove off. A perfect murder, a crime of passion is what he had called it.
Just on the outskirts of town he was singing along with the songs on the radio. His eyes were tired. His body was tired.
He felt the bite before he even saw her, felt the teeth sink into his skin and felt the blood spurting out as he lost control of the car.
No one in front of him and no one behind him the car went off into the ditch.
It wasn't going to be long before the blood drained out of him.
There she was, her teeth razor sharp.
He could see how dark her eyes were, she was dead, how could she attack him?
Gurgling noises came from his mouth, he could taste the blood that was coming up and spilling out over his lips.
His heart was racing, he tried to fight her off, letting go of the wheel in the last attempt to save his own life.

Shocked and horrified that she was eating him as if she was eating a steak. The more blood that came out the more she bit into him.

It wasn't long before his body was slumped over, his head against the window when the car stopped.

The windshield broken; the airbags had gone off.

She licked her lips. He had been the sweetest one yet. The best tasting and she wished that she had saved him for a snack instead of a meal.

"No one gets out alive." She whispered against his ear, knowing that he was completely dead before she stepped out of the car unharmed.

She pulled the ice pick out of chest, the blood disappearing as she disappeared into the night.

Hunting for the next that would taste as sweet as he did.

She walked into the foggy mist that was coming in during the early hours of morning. A smile on her face as she wiped the blood from around her mouth just to lick it off her hand.

There was no shame. It was a way she lived. If he had cared enough to ask who she truly was. She would have told him the truth.

No one ever wanted to ask her who she was. Sure, they knew her name, but not who she was. They were so easy to judge. So quick to think that she didn't care about anyone but herself.

She cared about survival, she cared about others. Some she could have pounced on.

She had compassion.

Other times, like tonight, she knew that she was starving when she felt his blood soaring through his veins. The way he held her so close. She knew he was strong, it meant that his blood was good.

Licking her lips one more time she giggled. The moon and the stars on the only things that saw what happened.

Ms. Innocent she called herself. She laughed louder as she continued walking down the side of the road.

The End

Description.

Sometimes dreams can be so real after seeing something in real life. Dreams so real you can taste the water. Ted knows the feeling of dreams turning into reality. He didn't realize how seeing a warning sign and ignoring it could turn so deadly. The taste of water in his mouth, the way the boy looked at him. It was only a dream, a horrible nightmare until Ted sees the reality of his dreams.

Swim

Ted knew how to swim. He knew how to swim since he was little. Being a lifeguard, for the third summer in a row he was making sure that everyone was out of the water. It was time to close up for the night. Another glorious day.

He was the only one left at the beach. At least he thought.

Scanning the water was when he saw someone bobbing out too far. Past the roped-off part of the beach.

"You're out too far! Come in!" He shouted out.

He couldn't tell if it was male or female, but he knew that they weren't supposed to be swimming out that far.

There was a drop-off. The ropes for the swimmer's safety.

Whoever it was wasn't coming in like he had told them to.

He knew it wasn't his job. After the beach closed down it was swim at your own risk, but he couldn't go home knowing that someone was out there. If something happened, he wouldn't be able to live with himself.

Blinking he looked out before taking off his shirt and the person was gone. He didn't know where they had gone but they were no longer there.

Scratching the back of his head, he couldn't understand it.

That night when he went to bed, he thought about the person out there in the water. Maybe they had swam

off to shore somewhere else. That's the only reasonable explanation that crossed his mind.
He drifted off to sleep.

There he was in the water, swimming and swimming to get to the person who was out beyond the ropes. He treaded water hollering out to them. They acted like they couldn't hear him.
That's when he saw the curly brown hair, a boy about his age. Teasing and taunting him.
"Swim. Swim. Swim." The boy kept calling.
No matter how fast Ted could swim he wasn't getting anywhere. He wasn't getting any closer to the boy.
"Come in." He called to him, waving his arm towards him.
The boy laughed and kicked water.
The boy stopped smiling; his body was going under. Ted sucked in his breath and went under the water, under the ropes. He reached out with his arm. He was inches away from the boy watching him go down, down, into the water.
The water was so dark he couldn't see him. He disappeared.

Ted woke up gasping, water coming out of his mouth. His body was sweating, his sheets were soaked as if he'd been in the water.
"What the hell." He whispered to himself, sitting on the edge of the bed and catching his breath. Where had the water come from that he'd been choking on?
"Swim. Swim. Swim." The boys voice came to him. Looking around his room no one was there.

He got a little more sleep before he went to work the next morning.

A smile on his face, forgetting about his dream.

There were crowds of people at the beach, he thought nothing of it until he got closer to his stand.

A boy about his age was there, he was laying there with his eyes closed.

"What is going on?" He asked one of the swimmers.

"He drowned. The drop off maybe. Someone dragged him out of the water." The person shrugged their shoulders.

He ran over to where the boy was. His curly brown hair. His body wet from the water. The boy that he'd seen in his dream. The person out beyond the ropes with only him there.

He felt himself drowning, gasping for air.

The boy opened, watery, brown eyes. His mouth opened. Blue as blue could be.

"Swim. Swim. Swim."

The End

Description

On his way home from a friend's, he cut through the woods. Never thinking that he would be a witness to screaming and horror. Instead of going home he stood behind the tree. He continued to watch in horror at what he could see. A strange man in the woods, a shack, a boy on a bench. He didn't know what was going on and maybe it was too late to help but he couldn't move. He couldn't do anything but watch and stare. What he didn't realize was if he didn't leave soon there'd be no escape.

Stranger

Never talk to a stranger. Stranger danger is what they were taught. Being a teenager now he thought it was funny. No stranger had ever come to him.
Walking home from a friend's house through the woods he heard a scream. Hearing a saw going and then stopping.
Another scream.
He was getting closer and closer to the noise. It sounded like someone in extreme pain and he felt his stomach turning.
Standing behind a tree he saw a small shack. He should've left, he should've turn and ran while he had the chance.
He was curious.
Standing behind the tree he saw someone on the bench outside. Tied down, his heart racing he wanted to move. He wanted to run; his feet wouldn't let him. He couldn't take his eyes off what was happening.
A big man came out of the shack, smiling and laughing.
"Who are you?" The boys voice asked, trying to struggle to get up.
He couldn't.
"Don't you know it's never nice to talk to strangers? Didn't your parents ever teach you that?" The man laughed.
He was a tall, burly, man. Red hair. The boy stood behind the tree. Making sure to get a good description.

He could at least give that to the police. Even if he couldn't help the boy on the bench.

The saw came down again, he saw blood, he heard the boy screaming. The screams that he'd heard walking through the woods.

He looked behind him, no one was coming. He didn't even take the woods. This was the first time in a long time he had come through them by himself.

He watched as the boy's arms were sawed off. Watched as his legs were getting cut off. How could someone do that to another human being?

He didn't know, he knew it was time to get out of there, he knew it was time to leave.

The saw stopped. The silence was strange to the boy's ears.

Why wasn't the boy on the bench screaming? Why wasn't he trying to get up?

Was he dead?

He licked his lips and continued to stare. Hoping that the boy was still alive; if he was, he wasn't going to be for long.

Breathing heavily the sun was going down, he should've been home hours ago. His phone in his pocket, he was surprised that his mother hadn't called him yet.

She should be on her way home from work. Just pulling in the driveway.

He thought about his mother, thought about the boy that was on the bench.

He wasn't paying attention to anything else.

That's when he felt a hand on his shoulder.

He jumped.

Looked at the shadow that was hanging over his own where the sun was hitting. Looking up slowly he could see that the man was much bigger than he was. "Didn't your parents ever teach you to mind your own business?" A man the boy didn't know asked him.

His voice was deep, his laugh even deeper as he felt the man pulling him away from the tree. Bringing him down closer and closer to the boy on the bench!

That's when his phone rang. He only had time to see who was calling.

His mother.

The stranger laughed as he took the phone and tossed it into the woods.

"You won't need this where you're going."

The boy on the bench was still alive, he watched the boy's chest move up and down.

"You're next." The stranger whispered in his ear and sat him down in a wooden chair. A front row seat for the live show.

The End

Description

It was a normal night of babysitting. An easy job, she would put the baby down and the rest of the night she could do whatever she wanted. That was until someone called continuously. A night of watching movies was turning into a night of terror for her. There were no neighbors that she could call, no one close by to ask for help. Her parents gone she's not sure if she can survive the scare that she receives. It's a night she will never forget…

Caller

She was babysitting for the neighbors, the only other people on the street. Woods on either side of the road. It was an ordinary night of movies and ice cream. She would wait until the little one went to bed before she put in the really good movies. The scary movies.
She got her snacks ready, got the drinks ready. She already had a bed-time story for the baby, and she would lay him in his crib to let him sleep.
It was easy and she got paid well for it.
After her routine she went back downstairs to start the horror movie. Her drinks and popcorn on the stand in front of her.
Just as the movie started, she heard the phone ring.
"Hello." She asked into the phone.
Heavy breathing, nothing but heavy breathing.
"I think you have the wrong number. This is the Henderson's residence." She said calmly and hung up the phone.
It wasn't long before the phone started to ring again.
"What do you want?" She asked.
"I know you're there alone." The voice was raspy.
"Stop." Her voice was calm, but inside she was already scared.
"Do you want me to show you?" The caller asked.
Before she could answer him, the light in the kitchen flickered off and on.
The caller was in the house!
She hung up the phone and got off the couch.

Heading up the stairs quickly she went into the baby's room and closed the door quietly. Trying to look for a way out.

There was the roof, but she had to climb onto it. She wasn't sure if she could even jump down with the baby.

The phone in her hand rang again.

"Please, leave." She began to cry when she picked up the phone.

"There's nowhere to go, nowhere to hide." He laughed into the phone.

"Why are you doing this?" She whined.

"Because I can." He laughed evilly and he was the one who hung up this time.

She took the baby out of the crib, carrying him to the window she slid it open. Getting herself out first and then the baby.

The baby stared at her, no confusion. No fussing.

Stepping out, the phone rang again.

She ignored it.

Why weren't her parents home yet? Where were they?

Pressing herself against the house so she wouldn't be seen, the phone continued to ring and ring.

She refused to answer the phone. She didn't want to play this game anymore.

It was then that she was about to jump down and take her chances. It was then that she thought she had no choice until she saw the Henderson's car pulling in the driveway.

They raced into the house.

"You guys came home early." She cried when she got back in through the window.

"You weren't picking up the phone. The phone was busy. Just as we were headed into town, we heard about someone calling random people. Whoever picked up would be found dead. We raced here…" Mrs. Henderson stated quickly, taking the baby.
The caller. She didn't want to tell them, she didn't have to.
They could see it on her face, the sweat, the tears.
"Call the police." She told them, walking out of the bedroom, trying to calm herself down.
She had come close to becoming a victim. Had come close to never going home again which was just a few feet away.
Mr. Henderson searched the house, finding no signs of anyone breaking in. No phone calls. The police would be able to search but they would find nothing.

The End

Description

He was starving, he couldn't stop thinking about food. Sitting out there in the cold. There was a reason he was hiding out there. He couldn't be seen in the public eye. He couldn't be noticed. Hearing the wolves made his mouth drool. It was when he heard voices that he was alarmed. When he saw her, he saw it more like a blessing in disguise. Something that he'd never thought before, he thought more about it as he saw her produce the lighter when she sat down beside him.

Hunger.

The red beady eyes staring out from the bushes. How cold it was, he couldn't remember the last time he had something to eat. He could hear the wolves howling, baying at the moon and he had thought about going after one of them. He knew that they traveled in packs. He had no tent, no fire to cook the meat on. There was no way that he was going to be able to eat raw animal meat.

Almost a week with no food. He had checked the traps. Nothing. He had the supplies for a fire, just nothing to light it with.

That's when he heard the arguing. A girl crying as she ran away from whoever was yelling at her. He licked his lips. Hearing her come closer and closer. She stopped when she saw him.

A beautiful blonde, she didn't say anything.

"Sit." He spoke, nodding his head at the snowbank that he was sitting by.

"What are you doing out here?" She asked, wiping the tears from her face.

He didn't answer her.

He watched as she took a pack of cigarettes out of her pocket. A lighter.

His eyes fixed on the lighter.

How was he going to get it?

"What's going on up there?" He asked, looking in the direction that she had come from.

"My boyfriend, such a loser." She rolled her eyes, took a drag and let it out.

He nodded his head as if he understood. He didn't though.
He could see that she was irritated. Soon she would calm down and go back to him, that's how his mother had been.
Always going back to the one who hurt them.
"I'm not going back. This is it." She shook her head as if she could read her thoughts.
"That's what they all say." He scoffed, not believing a word she said.
He looked over her body.
She blushed.
It wasn't a compliment. He was hungry, he wasn't thinking straight. He had no way of eating he couldn't be seen.
If they saw him, they would lock him up.
"Want one?" She asked him, handing him the cigarettes.
He wasn't a smoker. Never liked the taste of it, the smell of it. He wanted that lighter though. His eyes glued to it.
He nodded his head and she gave him them both to him.
His hands were shaking when he took the cigarette out of the pack. It was now or never. He brought it to his lips and lit the end of the cigarette.
It was in the glow of the lighter that she gasped. She knew he was. Everyone knew who he was. The serial killer.
His face had been all over the news.
With one swift motion he got up from where he was, she tried to scream but she wasn't as fast as he was.

Taking her neck, he snapped it with ease. Watching her mouth stay frozen in a shocked expression.
He waited.
Nothing.
Silence. Just like he'd hoped.
No one had heard the struggle. He highly doubted that she realized what was happening to her until the last second.
He sat back down. There was no blood. He let her body stay like that for a few minutes.
He had no emotion running through him.
Starving he took the lighter.
It took a few minutes before the clothing would light.
They were too far away for anyone to see.
If her boyfriend was home, he was sure no one was looking out the windows. He couldn't even see the house from where he was sitting on the bank.
Wolves still howling at the moon.
He watched as her body began to turn charcoal before he began to pack the body with ice, putting the fire out little by little.
He closed his eyes and bit into the burnt skin. Tasting the meat. His mouth almost drooling from the taste.
He sat there and ate her like she was a Thanksgiving turkey. The only thing he wished for was hot sauce and he knew that he should be thankful for what he had.
It was the feeling of starvation that had made him do it. He was hiding out.
If she hadn't realized who he was she would still be laying there. Since he caught sight of the lighter, he knew what he was going to do.

Only the strongest survived and that's why he was still here.

The End

Description

She'd always liked the dark, there was nothing better than letting it consume her when she was having a rough time. It was her net. That was until one night everything changed. She would no longer be the woman she had once been. Never again welcoming the dark with open arms.

Darkness.

She didn't think anything of it, laying in the field across the street from her house it was quiet, it was peaceful. A smile on her face as she looked up at the stars. They were shining brightly that night, she had such a rough day and it was the best place for her to be.
Sometimes she would lay there, and she would feel like she was on a different planet. She didn't have to think.
Looking over at her house it was dark. She didn't want to go back home. She wanted to run away from everything in life but knew that she couldn't, she had too many responsibilities.
It was harder to walk away when she had so many things that had to be done.
Sighing heavily, she got up and walked slowly back to the house.
As she walked up the driveway she felt as if something was the matter.
She brushed it off.
Walking into the house she tried turning on the light.
Nothing.
The house was quiet. A little too quiet.
She could hear the faucet dripping into the empty sink.
Walking further into the house she found herself breathing in and out slowly.
Something got knocked over in the living room.
She heard it crash to the floor.
A lamp. The bulb.

"Damn cat." She whispered to herself.
Walking into the living room she didn't see anything. It was when she headed upstairs that she felt something go around her waist. She felt herself being carried away from the stairs.
A set of arms.
She tried to kick and scream, she felt her heart racing. She slammed her head back, but nothing happened. Whoever had her, wasn't going to let her go.
A hand covered her mouth and nose. She couldn't breathe!
She had to remain calm, her mind was racing. Her body sweating.
She was being taken out of the house.
Brought to a car around the side of the house!
The trunk opened and was thrown inside.
Gasping for air, sucking in the cool night air she didn't have a chance to get out of the trunk before the lid closed.
She laid in there, trying to estimate how much time she had before she lost breathing room.
She never had to think like this.
It was dark, the kind of dark that she normally liked. Not tonight.
It smelled of death. Stale air and she didn't find any peace in it, she didn't find the comfort in the darkness.
It had been torn from her, the fear was creeping in.
Closing her eyes, she tried to find her relax spot. She had to think.
She tried to think about the field. How good it made her feel, how she felt like nothing could touch her. She couldn't find it.

The bumps in the road made her hit her head off the top of the trunk and it hurt. She felt dizzy. Trying to breathe.

The car stopped. She sucked in her breath and kept her eyes closed.

The trunk opened.

"Today's your lucky day." The voice was jumbled. She couldn't tell if she knew the person or not.

They wore a ski-mask and she couldn't tell who it was.

She didn't even know what they were talking about. The person got back in the car and left her there. Driving off into the night.

There were no streetlights. There was no light at all to go by.

Falling on her hands and knees she felt her shoulders shaking. She felt the tears come to her eyes and felt them slipping out.

She stayed there in the middle of the road in the dark night until she couldn't cry anymore. Until her eyes hurt, and her head was pounding.

Getting on her feet she walked in the direction of home.

Seeing the darkness for what it was.

It wasn't peaceful, it wasn't there to make anyone secure but to make them alert in the post horrifying ways.

She didn't know who the man had been, but he had stripped her of what she liked the most. The darkness helped her when she couldn't handle life anymore.

Every noise on the way home made her jump. She was spooked when she should've felt comforted by the darkness that surrounded her.

Looking up in the sky, not even the stars, that were shining brightly just for her, looked the same. She would never look at the darkness the way she once had.

She was relieved to see her house come into view. The lights were still out.

Never had she thought about keeping a light on in case she was going to be home late. It never crossed her mind.

Seeing her house in complete darkness she froze where she was. Her heart was pounding so loudly she could feel the vibration in her head.

The tears started flowing again as she slowly walked to the front porch. She looked around, not seeing anyone or anything.

Taking the steps once at a time, her steps even slower now she opened the door.

Feeling along the wall with her hand she was relieved when she felt the light switch and it turned on bringing the light to her.

She stepped into the house and locked the door behind her.

It was a night that changed her life forever.

Never again would she walk through the darkness by herself again.

She would always have someone with her no matter who it was.

She felt the change inside of her.

Wiping away the tears she turned on the big light in the living room and grabbed the blanket from the back of the couch.

Staring at the staircase that led upstairs everything came back to her in an instant. The way the fear had gripped her. The way the man had gripped her. That feeling would never go away, she gripped her pillow and kept her eyes open as long as she could.

The End

Description.

Can you keep a secret? Are you a trustworthy person? If someone was to tell you their deepest, darkest secret would you keep it or turn on them? Some secrets being told could kill you if you're not careful. Be watchful of the friends. Of the secrets that they want to tell you and never, ever break that trust because you never know if you're being tested. Maggie had a secret, a big one and when it came out, she wasn't sure who she could trust. She wasn't sure if she could even trust her friend Linda. Maggie wasn't sure that she could trust anyone anymore. Not even the one friend she had grown up with.

Can You Keep A Secret?

That's what her best friend Maggie asked her. If she could keep a secret? She didn't know what kind of secret she had, but she could see that Maggie's eyes were red from crying.

They were in their favorite spot. High up in the pine tree. It's where they had gone when they were little. Now they were in their late teens and they still climbed the tree when they wanted to get away from everyone.

"You know that I can." She looked at her, not knowing why Maggie would ask such a thing.

"It happened last night." She whispered as if they were in a crowded room.

"What did?" She looked at Maggie as if she had two heads. Confusion setting in.

"They were fighting. The blood, there was a lot of blood. I didn't know what to do. I didn't know what to say. They are dead." Maggie was keeping it together well.

It was as if she was telling a story for someone else and not herself.

"Linda?" Maggie asked.

Linda stared at her.

"I'm listening." She whispered, not sure what she was going to hear next.

"I don't know what happened. I walked in on it. I didn't see anyone. It was the terrifying sight. I ran, ran far away and called you to meet me here."

Maggie looked at her hands.

There were blood stains on her hands.

She was staring down at them.

Linda didn't dare to say anything to her. She didn't want to break Maggie's train of thought. She had to get it out.

"The blood, it's theirs." Maggie didn't feel like crying. Even if she wanted to, she wouldn't be able to.

Her heart was racing.

The feeling that came over her.

"Who did it?" Linda finally asked.

She stared at Maggie's hands.

"Me. But it wasn't me. It was like I was watching myself do it. An out-of-body experience, that's what it felt like." Maggie nodded her head

Linda had thought she didn't know who did it.

That's what Maggie had said.

But Maggie wasn't in her right mind, she knew that now.

Linda didn't know what to say.

For the first time she didn't know what to say to her best friend that she'd known since they were just kids.

"Maggie." Linda whispered.

She wanted to reach out to her friend. She wanted to comfort her, but she didn't know how to. She wasn't scared of her.

Maggie wasn't being Maggie. She wasn't the same girl now, but that didn't mean Linda was going to judge her.

"Do you know what?" Maggie asked.

"What?" Linda asked.

"I don't think that you can keep a secret." Maggie was so calm when she shoved Linda so hard that she fell off the tree branch.

She watched as Linda screamed all the way down. Watched as her body hit the ground, her head bouncing off a rock.

There was no doubt in her mind that Linda was dead. A small smile came to her face. She felt like she was untouchable. The power that she felt in the moment. The rush is what made her do it. The more control she had the better she felt. There was nothing more than the feeling of power.

Slowly Maggie made it down the tree in one piece. Using each thick branch as a step like they had done when they were little.

They had helped each other they had trusted each other.

Linda never should've trusted her, never should've climbed the tree with her.

That's what trust did.

It got you killed and now Linda couldn't speak a word even if she wanted to.

Walking over to her body she crouched down and lifted Linda's head off the rock. No one was going to find her. It would be weeks and by then the animals would take care of her. Nothing to find.

Linda's lifeless eyes stared at her accusingly.

Maggie smiled at her as if they were still friends.

"Dead people tell no tales." She whispered and closed Linda's eyes for the last time.

She stayed there cradling Linda until the sun was setting behind the trees as if it had seen what Maggie had done and kept a silent promise that it wouldn't tell a soul.

She stayed until it got darker and darker.

Hearing branches breaking on the ground. She smiled.

A pack of wolves had come out for a late-night snack. "Come and get it." She whispered to them.

She stood up and stepped away from Linda's body. She climbed the tree a safe distance away from the wolves and watched as they devoured her best friend. She watched until they looked up at her, licking their bloodied chops. Watched as they turned and went back into the woods.

"There's more where that came from." Maggie finally told them and watched them disappear into the dark.

The End

Description

Have you ever looked in the mirror and think that maybe someone was on the other side? Another person watching you but you not being able to see them. Chelsea's life is about to change. Never once realizing until she sees a shadow. She sees brown eyes looking back at her. At first, she thinks she's going crazy. Until she hears the banging on the other side…

In the Mirror

Chelsea was straightening her blonde hair, layering it her blue eyes were trained on her face. On her hair. A smile that could make the sun shy away from its brightness.
Out of the corner of her eye she saw a shadow in the mirror. Jumping back and burning her finger on the straightener, she looked again, and it was gone.
She turned around nothing was there.
Shaking her head and glaring at herself she started doing her hair again.
Not enough sleep would do that to a person. Seeing things that really weren't there. She was sure she was going crazy.
After about fifteen minutes she was done fixing her hair.
Chelsea stared into the mirror, getting closer and closer to it to make sure her makeup was right. Her blue eyes shining back.
"What was that?" She gasped, the closer her eyes got to the mirror the more she saw brown eyes instead of light blue.
That had never happened to her before.
A light knock on the bathroom door made her jump back.
Turning away from the mirror she did see the fingers that were pushing through. Quickly they disappeared when the knock rang through.
"Almost done! Go away!" Chelsea shouted at her younger brother as she unlocked and opened the bathroom door.

"Well, you've been in there for hours." He grunted, rolling his eyes and turning away.

She slammed the bathroom door and leaned against it, closing her eyes and taking a deep breath.

She laughed at herself.

Chelsea had thought that the knock came from the mirror.

The brown eyes though, she knew she wasn't seeing things. She just knew it.

Looking at the bathroom door and back at the mirror she went back to the mirror to see if she could see the eyes again.

In the darkness, in the other side of the mirror, she saw the girl. She heard the muffled voices. She couldn't hear what they were saying but she could tell that they were talking.

How nice it would be to switch places, to finally be free. All the girl had to do was come a little closer. She knew that she had been seen. It was a gateway that not many people had.

"Please see me." The girl in the mirror whispered. Chelsea was fixing her makeup. She was more intent on herself than what went beyond her own image.

"See me!" She yelled, banging her fists on the mirror.

Chelsea jumped back this time. The pounding was coming from the mirror! Her heart racing, she inched closer and closer to the mirror.

That's when it happened.

The arms reached out!

Chelsea tried screaming, she tried to pull back away from the mirror, but she couldn't.

Pushing herself away from the sink with her knees she knew that she was in trouble when her head went through the mirror like going through a portal.
She saw the girl on the other side.
"See me. I am here. Trapped behind the mirror." The girl's nails were digging into her shoulders. Pulling her in more and more.
The girl's hair was chopped. Her brown eyes now turning a reddish tint. When the girl opened her mouth, she could see that they were jagged and sharp. The girl pulled Chelsea in until she was all the way inside. She had only a few seconds to jump through the mirror.
"Now you are the one in there until someone sees you." The girl laughed, her image looking exactly like Chelsea's.
The red eyes turned to blue. Chelsea tried everything, beating her hands against the mirror on the other side. The dark side.
"HELP!" Chelsea screamed out loud.
No one could hear her.
She could see the girl leaving the bathroom looking just like her!
Then she saw her brother come into the bathroom.
It would be the only way she'd see her family again. They wouldn't realize that the Chelsea they saw wasn't her!
Trapped forever in the darkness, for Chelsea wasn't going to do what the girl in the mirror had done. She wouldn't be able to take someone's place. She wouldn't be able to be that selfish. It would stop with her.

The End.

Description

The night shift at the morgue isn't the best job in the world, but it's a job and that's the way she sees it. No one else is crazy enough to take the shift or the money that goes with it. There are reasons why we don't do things that are scary. Sometimes you don't get out alive!

The Morgue

The body was on the slab in the middle of the room. She was the only one working that night. The only one crazy enough to work with dead bodies in the middle of the night. No one wanted the night shift, but it paid good money.
Checking the freezer trays she didn't know why she was doing it. Dead bodies couldn't move but when she opened the last one it was empty.
There was supposed to be a male body in there.
Hearing the swinging doors slide open she jumped.
"I took him to get cleaned up before tomorrow." Brandon told her.
Brandon was the guy that would only stay a few minutes. Most times he wouldn't even go inside the room, just leaving the body outside the door for her to take.
"I wish you would tell me before you take them." She sucked in her breath and let it out slowly.
"What's the matter, night shift getting to you?" He laughed at her.
She didn't laugh, she rolled the body over onto the tray and pushed the drawer shut.
As soon as Brandon left though she wished that she could convince him to stay.
The lights in the morgue kept flickering. It was an old building; it had happened to her a hundred times before. Something she was used to.
Finally, it was time for her nightly break. She didn't eat when she was in the morgue.
When she came back it was dark, the lights were out.

She flicked the switch off and on and nothing.
"Jesus." She muttered to herself.
That's when she heard it.
Drawers opening and closing. Opening and closing.
Her eyes adjusted to the darkness, she should've run, but she couldn't make her feet move. She tried pushing against the swinging doors and now they wouldn't budge!
The closer the bodies got to her the more she tried to scream. Someone had to be down on the floor.
She was never completely alone.
She felt the hands; she felt the coldness of the dead. The clammy coldness as she pushed her head back away from them. Trying to escape through the door that wouldn't swing open.
"Help me! Somebody." She thought she was screaming. It came out as a whispered whimper.
She felt them biting her, eating her!
In the morning there would be nothing but bones to state that she was there. No one would be prepared for the way she looked.
She didn't want to die like this. She never thought of dying like this.
Dead bodies coming alive, not looking like zombies. Looking like just dead people that were made up and taken care of.
She cried as they took her down to the floor.
One of the last things she saw was the last freezer tray opening.
The light flickered off and on.
Looking into the light as she felt her body growing numb, she prayed for the next person who was stupid enough to take on the night shift.

The day shift would have to pick straws. Whoever got the shortest one would end up like her!
The next morning all the bodies were back in the freezer trays tucked away in the drawers. Brandon was the one who found her, dropping the folder that he had in his hands he ran out of the morgue screaming…
He'd never seen such a sight. He didn't have to take a close look to see that it was her. Who would do such a horrific thing? He didn't know but that would be the last time he'd ever go down to the morgue.

The End

Description.

It was a harmless game of truth or dare. Kyle didn't even want to play it, he wanted truth. His friends convinced him to pick dare. One of the worst things that you could ever do in a graveyard is to play truth or dare, let alone touch a headstone that doesn't belong to you. You leave the dead alone or face the revenge they seek.

Truth or Dare

That's how it started that night. Kyle's friends had decided it would be fun to play truth or dare in a graveyard.

Kyle wanted to pick truth. His friends teased him until he finally caved in and chose dare, just to shut them up.

"Take the ruby off this headstone." His friend Andrew laughed.

"I'm not doing that." Kyle shook his head.

"You have to, it's a dare." He pointed out to Kyle.

"I don't have anything to take it out with." He grunted.

Andrew took out his pocket-knife that he always kept sharpened.

"It probably won't even come out." Kyle rolled his eyes, taking the pocket-knife.

He jumped off the headstone and stood in front of it. He couldn't see the name on the stone.

It was just a stupid dare.

He slid the point of the blade behind the ruby and, just like Andrew said it, popped out without an issue. Holding it in his hand he felt the burning sensation like his hand was on fire. He felt the burn against his palm as he continued to hold it.

"Fuck!" He shouted, dropping it.

"What's the matter with you?" Andrew asked.

The ruby was on the ground in front of them.

Andrew picked it up and felt the coolness of it.

He gave it back to Kyle. It wasn't hot anymore.

It wasn't long before they all went home. Everyone but Kyle.
Kyle leaned against the headstone.
Ruby in his hand; he felt it again.
He watched his hand turn orange like embers. The pain soaring through his hand and up his arm.
The burn was spreading and as hard as he tried Kyle couldn't take the ruby out of his hand. He couldn't shake it.
Screaming at the top of his lungs he leaned his head against the stone. The fiery sensation was getting stronger and stronger.
Looking at the headstone, seeing it clearly.

To those who take the ruby there will be a fiery warning the first time. There is no warning the second.

That's all it said, no name under it. No date of birth and date of death.
Kyle was getting it, he was understanding it, but only when it was too late.
His body began to cool and when he was turning to stone. The pain was worse than the burn. As the stone cooled on his body he began to turn to dust.
It wasn't long before the sun came up and a gust of wind blew Kyle's ashes away. The ruby back in its rightful place.
For years they put up missing persons reports on telephone poles, on stores' windows in hopes that they would find Kyle eventually.
No one knew where he could be.

Andrew visited the graveyard often, remembering the night, wondering how the ruby had been put back in the stone that he had dared Kyle to take it out of.
He had reached for the ruby numerous times but never touched it. He came close just a finger away from seeing if it would come out.
Each time something brought him away from it.
He would never tell anyone what he truly thought happened to Kyle. He read the stone all the time. Remembered Kyle dropping the ruby and crying out in pain.
Stranger things have happened, but once in a while he could hear Kyle's whispered voice in his ear.
The only words that Andrew heard from Kyle over and over again.

Don't touch it. Look what happened to me Andrew, don't touch it.

The End

Description

Have you ever wished for something and it came true, but not the way you wanted them to? Wishes are supposed to be magical they're supposed to bring you happiness when they are granted but careful what you wish for the outcome you may not like. Careful what you wish for. You just might have them answered but in the scariest form. Never once thinking that your wishes could be harmful to others, or even more tragic, harmful to yourself. Careful what you wish for, you just might get it.

Three Wishes.

He found it out in the woods. Tripped over it. He had never seen an antique lamp before. There was something he couldn't read on the side of it.
He waited until he got home and rushed up to his room. Taking a towel, he rubbed the dust off it, and before he knew it, there was a red cloud coming through the opening of the lamp.
A filmy gray figure came out of the lamp. A very small one.
He jumped back on the bed.
"Who are you?" His voice shaking.
"You have three wishes. Any three you want." The voice was deep and dark.
Scary.
But he had the wishes ready to roll off his tongue.
"Don't waste them." The gray figure wasn't smiling.
That should've been his first warning.
"I wish for tomorrow's test to be cancelled." He grinned.
In one of his college classes he hadn't studied for the test and he knew that he was going to fail. He just needed a little more time.
"Done." The gray figure grinned.
The television in his room turned on by itself and his eyes went to it.
There was an accident. The car he recognized.
His anatomy's Professor's car.
No survivors.
He heard the figure laugh evilly.
"That's not what I meant!" He shouted.

The test would be cancelled forever. No one else knew how to teach that class and they wouldn't find another so quickly before classes were done for the school year.

"I made your wish come true. Two more." The gray figure wasn't smiling anymore.

He shook his head; he wasn't going to.

"If you don't make two more, you will be the one trapped in here." The gray figure glared at him.

He tried to think of a wish that wasn't going to hurt anyone.

"I wish for a dog." There was no way that he could go wrong with that.

"Done." The gray figure laughed again.

There was barking outside.

He went to the window and saw a junkyard dog, his teeth so sharp that he was sure one bite would break a bone.

He glared at the figure.

"Soon someone will be coming through that gate. Who comes home after you?" The figure asked.

His eyes grew wide. His mother would be coming home. He got a sick feeling in his stomach. He had to think quickly.

His mind racing, he wasn't sure that he could come up with one that would save his mother.

"I wish for the dog to be out of my yard!" He yelled the last wish out.

The gray figure laughed and laughed.

"Done." He said between his laughter.

The growl was low and deep. It was so close to him.

Looking over his shoulder he saw the dog at his bedroom door. He saw that it wasn't a junkyard dog at all. It was a hellhound.

He had heard of hellhounds before, but he never thought that they existed.

It had blood dripping for fur. It had teeth so big that they could take off his whole arm. The wishes he had wanted ran deep.

The hellhound pounced, knocking him down.

"Help me!" He shouted.

"I'm sorry, you are out of wishes." The gray figure grew and grew until it was floating over him watching the show.

His eyes grew wide as he felt the teeth sink into his throat. The pain was horrible, he couldn't scream, blood squirting everywhere.

The hellhound didn't stop until there was nothing left of him.

The gray figure closed its eyes. Nothing remained in the room.

Not the boy. Not the hellhound and not the lamp.

The End

Description

Halloween is supposed to be the best time of the year. The only time of the year you can scare someone and get away with it. Sometimes the scare lasts for a few minutes and sometimes the scare lasts for hours maybe even a lifetime depending on who you are. Depending on what scared you to begin with.

Killer Mask

It was Halloween and Jamie had worked hard to get the mask that he wanted. It was the newest one. A black mask that promised to be like a second skin. He tried it on and took it off. He'd done this several times as he got into the black suit that came with it.
"Are you ready yet?" His friend Tommy asked.
They were too old for trick or treating. They were handing out candy instead, and Jamie wanted to scare the little kids who came ringing the doorbell before giving them candy.
It was Halloween. Everyone liked being scared.
"Yeah, I'm ready." He put the mask back on and headed down the stairs.
The doorbell rang.
Jamie laughed.
"The first of many trick or treaters!" He shouted, grabbing the bowl of candy off the table and heading for the door.
There was one little boy. He could see that his mother was standing at the end of the driveway. He held out his bucket.
"Roar!!!" Jamie shouted, one hand up in the air. His eyes couldn't be seen through the mask.
The little boy's eyes grew wide as he jumped back. He dropped his bucket and ran across the yard to his mother.
The boy's mother gave him a dirty look and shook her head.
"What? I didn't think that it was that bad." Jamie looked at Tommy.

Tommy stared at the mask. His eyes growing wide.
"What?" Jamie almost barked at him.
"Things, there are things coming out of the mask. Worms, maggots, I don't know." Tommy was terrified himself.
Jamie looked in the mirror in the hallway. There was nothing there.
"Nice try." He grunted, shaking his head.
Tommy didn't say anything, they were gone. How could he explain it to Jamie that they were gone?
Throughout the night Jamie scared more and more trick or treaters; some stayed for the candy while others ran away.
He felt something inside his mask, something crawling. He tried taking it off a few times, but he couldn't manage to get it off his face.
Sweat, that's all he could think of.
He wasn't going to worry about it, though maybe he should've.
It was almost time to go in for the night. Halloween was almost over.
That's when he felt the sharp pains against his face.
"Tommy!" He cried out, turning towards Tommy who was getting ready to put the rest of the candy away.
"What the hell!?" Tommy shouted.
"What's going on?" Jamie was scared, the pain was almost unbearable.
"Blades, there are blades pushing in and out of your mask!" Tommy shouted he couldn't reach for them; he didn't want to get cut up.
"Help me, help me get it off." Jamie was crying.

Tommy tried to tug on the sides of the mask, but nothing happened.

Just more agonizing screams coming from Jamie.

"You're tearing my skin. I can feel it, stop!" Jamie shouted.

"Where the hell did you get this mask? I can't get it off you." Tommy was panicking. Not sure how he could get it off Jamie without hurting him.

"A small shop. More like a gypsy shop." He grunted, thinking it was the best thing.

The blades continued to dig through his skin. He felt it teasing his bones.

"Did she say anything? Did the woman say anything?" Tommy was trying to think of how he might be able to help.

"Once it goes on it will never come off. She laughed, I thought she was just trying to scare me. It is Halloween you know." He cried uncontrollably that Tommy could barely understand him.

"There's no way to get it off then." Tommy's heart was racing.

It was then that Jamie fell to the ground. Hitting his head off the stone stairs. Tommy tried helping him back up, but he could see that Jamie wasn't moving. He wasn't breathing.

"Jamie!" Tommy shouted in his ear.

Maybe he wasn't dead, maybe he was unconscious, but he knew even then, breathing would continue.

It was now or never.

Tommy pulled on both sides of Jamie's mask. Pulling harder and harder he felt it loosen little by little.

"It's coming off Jamie! I'm able to get it off!"
Tommy shouted with excitement thinking that he was helping.
It wasn't until the mask was finally freed from his friends face that Tommy realized there had been no helping Jamie.
Even if the mask didn't come off.
When the mask came off it had taken Jamie's face with it. Skin and flesh. Looking closer he saw where the blades had drilled into Jamie's head.
Jamie should've been dead hours ago it seemed by the looks of the maggots surrounding the holes that were made in Jamie's face. The stabbing marks going all the way to the back of his head to where Tommy could see the other side.
Someone had called an ambulance Tommy knew it was too late and it was the last time that he'd ever spoken.
He thinks about that Halloween night behind the thick windows of the insane hospital room; everyone had blamed him when it came to Jamie's death.
Everyone believed if someone could do something like that to their best friend. They weren't in their right mind.
Tommy never cleared it up for anyone. How could he? No one would believe him. It was as if it had happened yesterday, as Tommy thought about his friend with tears sliding down his face.
Every Halloween he wonders if it really happened or if it was just a dream that he was reliving again and again.

The End

Description.

The sign said keep out. No one ever listened to the warnings. The abandoned prison was a sight to see though. The only sight that anyone would see once they entered. The second they went in they didn't know that there was no coming out. The sign was there for a reason. For the safety. Secrets were held in the abandoned prison. Remains of inmates who got what they deserved. Justice was served but the secret would never leave the prison walls.

Prisoner

They entered the old prison. Summer had just started.
It was an abandoned prison, just the two of them.
Kylie and Destiny.
"I don't know why we have to do this." Destiny grumbled.
It wasn't the highlight of her day.
"I want to see what it looks like on the inside." Kylie whined at her.
Kylie was for adventure and Destiny was not.
They went through the gate. There was no turning back now.
The rusted metal sign "Keep out." Didn't keep them out.
Walking up and down the cell blocks it didn't take Destiny long to see that she wanted to get out of there.
"Look!" She cried out, her voice echoing off the walls.
There were human remains in one of the cells and the more they passed they saw remains of some even clinging to the bars.
"You'd think that someone would clean these out." Destiny was shaking. She'd never seen human bones before.
They went to the office where the warden would be if it wasn't abandoned.
Going through the drawers Kylie found papers that stated the deaths.
The pictures were gruesome. There were pictures with the warden smiling next to the dead inmates.

"No one had called these in." Kylie gasped, her eyes growing wide.

"Cold-blooded murder." Destiny winced.

There was a loud banging sound. Like a metal cup running up and down the bars.

Someone was singing.

"Who could it be?" Destiny asked, whimpering.

She was scared.

Kylie was scared too but she wasn't going to admit it. She wasn't going to put Destiny in a panic attack.

"They come in, but they never come out. They come in and the never come out." The voice was getting closer. The clanging of the cup against the bars getting louder.

They ducked down under the desk, the door to the office opened and the girls held each other tightly.

"I know you're here. I heard you come in. The sign says keep out." Someone jumped onto the desk and looked down over the girls.

The warden!

Kylie knew who it was.

"The secret is out and now you can't leave. You couldn't leave the second you entered." The warden glared down at them.

"We won't tell anyone." Destiny began crying when the warden jumped off the desk with his phone in his hand.

He took the sword down off the wall that he liked to use. With one swift motion the blade came down over their heads.

Destiny's screams were cut off when she was decapitated. The warden put their heads on the desk and took a selfie.

"They come in, but they never come out." The warden continued to sing as he left the office and continued to wait for the next victims that were going to make the same mistake that they had.

They were all young teens. The ones that came in. Never once heeding the warning.

The warden whistled a happy tune as he continued to make his rounds. There was no one there, there would be by the time that he made his last round for the night.

It always happened that way. The prison was abandoned. No one to keep up on it. The secret of murder and what happened in the prison were always found out.

He couldn't let them leave; he couldn't risk anyone opening their mouths about the time spent at the prison.

Murder was what took place. According to the warden being behind bars wasn't justice. An eye for an eye and a tooth for a tooth.

The inmates were killed exactly how they killed their victims. The warden would never let the secret out.

The End

Description

Old stories and rumors about the house all the way down the street. The one that had been abandoned long before the recent neighbors had moved into the hood. They were made up stories no one could ever really tell what happened down in the basement. When it came to going inside of it everyone steered clear of it. The stories stopping them in their tracks except for one girl…

Basement.

No one was allowed to go down in the basement. It was locked up tight and only one person held the key. That one person long gone.

The house sat all the way down the block. No one ever went in and no one ever came out at least that's how the story went.

Every day Lisa would walk past the house to go to her friends. She would look at it, with its broken windows. Dust clinging to them.

They hadn't been washed in years. She found it crazy though that the basement windows looked brand-new washed inside and out.

She stopped in front of the house, standing there and staring at it as if she were in a trance, something she had never done before. She was sure that it was calling her name.

Hearing her name in the wind, there was no one around.

The clouds were coming in, soon it was going to rain, and she had to be home for dinner. The reason why she left her friend's house early.

She looked down the street to her house, counting them.

Five houses away.

She moved closer and closer to the house, wanting to go home but wanting to see what the story was.

She didn't believe in ghost stories, maybe she could prove to everyone there was nothing there. She would be the first one to come out of the house.

She laughed at the thought as she took a rock and broke the basement window easily. Glass layered the floor as she climbed in through the window.
It was empty. Well, almost empty.
There were dust prints on the floor. Not just any dust prints. Footprints. She should've taken it as a warning.
She followed them instead and it led her to a hole in the wall. Bricks had been taken out. Words were written on them.
"Dead but don't forget me. It's too late to leave. This is our home now." She read a few of them as she tossed them.
Taking out her cell phone she put the flashlight on.
Climbing into the hole was her second mistake.
Bones everywhere. Three or four people were in each corner of the spaces. She went to go turn away. Went to go climb out of the hole.
There was no hole!
It was just a wall. She pushed against it with all her might. It wasn't budging.
"Let me out!" She shouted, fear in her voice.

This is where they hide the dead bodies. The missing that assume just run away.

She pressed her back against the wall and shined her flashlight.
The bones were coming alive!

Soon you will be dead. We haven't had a sweet treat in a long time.

If she could have turned back time, she would've just walked away like everyone else. Pretended the house wasn't there.

It's lonely down here. For years we've been here with no one coming in to look for us. No one knows that we are here and soon you will be among the missing. They will stop looking for you. You will be able to hear them calling your name from the outside but try as you might no one will ever hear you. The screams of spirits don't exist to the outside world. We've been down here forever.

She tried again and again to push against the wall. The hole had to be there somewhere; it wasn't until late in the evening that she realized there was no escape.
Falling asleep was the worst thing she could've done. For she never woke up, she never got out to tell the story of what she had found. The murdered, the victims of long ago by the one who had owned the house. The reason why the basement always stayed locked.

The End

Description.

There was no doubt that his pet was hungry. It had been quite some time since he'd last fed it. He didn't feel sorry, not one little bit. He knew what he had to do, and he did it. A little selfish sure, but he refused to be a victim. He'd lived a long life and he would continue to live his life until his maker came for him, but it wouldn't be any time soon.

His Pet

His pet had to eat. It had been weeks since it had been fed and he knew that it was time. In his black car he waited patiently on the side of the road. It always happened the same way. Always needing a ride, a call to bring a person here or there.

He had been a cabby for twenty-three years.

It came across the scanner of where he needed to go just a few seconds after thinking about his pet.

With a grin on his face he went to the location and saw a heavy-set woman get in the backseat of the car.

"Where to?" He asked.

The woman huffed at him.

"Twenty-nine Mollison Way. It's on the outskirts of town." She turned her nose up.

This one was going to be fun; he could already sense it the second she got in.

The doors locked automatically.

She didn't say anything about it.

There was silence on the ride.

He continued to look in the mirror and saw that she was resting her head, relaxing during the ride.

It was only a few seconds later that he could hear her snoring lightly and that's when he hit the button.

The back of the car was getting misty, clouds of smoke.

He laughed just a little.

Sleeping gas. That's what it was, nothing too harmful. A little extra dosage so that when he had to wake her up, she would be coherent but not able to fight him.

He drove to his house, pulling into the driveway he unlocked the doors. She wouldn't wake up for a while.

He got the zip ties, tying her hands behind her back. He managed to get her out and put her in a wheelchair.

As he made his way down to the dock that led out to the lake, he whistled a cheerful tune. A tune that only one thing could be able to hear.

Hearing the slithering as he got closer and closer to the dock, he saw that his pet was almost out of the water.

Its tongue slipping in and out of its mouth, its eyes black and beady.

"It's been a while, I know." He told the snake that was much bigger than he was.

It eyed the chair as it came out of the water.

That's when he heard her scream.

"You're awake." He laughed.

Her eyes grew wider and wider, her screams louder and louder.

"Why are you doing this?" She began to cry when she realized she couldn't get out of the chair.

"That thing has been here since I was a kid. It'd almost eaten me once. I can't have that happen again. I would rather sacrifice others than myself." He whispered in her ear.

He pushed the wheelchair all the way down the dock and dumped her in the water. The woman made a huge splash.

The snake dove its head into the water and brought it back up quickly.

It tossed the woman up into the air and played with her as she screamed and cried.

"How many times do I have to tell you not to play with your food?" The man asked, glaring at the snake. As if it could understand what he was saying, the snake tossed the woman into the air one more time and the screams stopped.

The man could see her body sliding down the inside of the snake's mouth, he turned away to let his pet eat in peace.

"Better you than me." He whispered going back up into the driveway, getting back into the cab, driving off and waiting for his next victim.

The End

Description

He had a killer smile that no one knew about. A boy who never smiled. The one time he did was terrifying. Not only for him but for a friend of his. The boy, now an old man, would never smile. Convinced he would hurt someone. Reliving that day over and over again in his head. Driving himself crazy. Maybe he would test it again and get a different result. Maybe it was all in his head just like his mother had told him so many years ago.

Smile.

Kevin didn't have a normal life growing up. He didn't smile. Everyone told him that he should, but the ones that he loved he couldn't smile around.
He stayed in his room, even now as an old man, he stayed in his room. He had smiled one time. Just once when he was growing up.
It was horrible. His smile had killed his best friend. Literally.

Seven years old was when it happened. He had taken his best friend Chris fishing just down the street from where they lived. It was something they'd always done.
"How come you never smile?" Chris asked him, throwing his line out in the water.
"I don't know, there's never a reason to." He shrugged his shoulders he had never once felt like smiling.
Even as a baby his mother said that he didn't smile. All of his pictures were thin-lipped. His teeth never showing.
Chris let it go, they talked about the fun times that they'd had fishing with each other. The challenge had always been whoever caught the biggest fish was the master fisherman.
Time had gotten away from them, soon the sun was setting, and they were packing up to go home knowing that they were going to get into trouble because they hadn't checked in.

"It wouldn't kill you to smile. I think that it might bring character to your face." Chris joked with him. Nudging him as they began their walk up the dock. It was then that their eyes met, that Kevin did smile. Chris's eyes grew wide. He dropped his tackle box. Kevin could see that something was wrong right away.

He stopped smiling as soon as Chris's face grew white and he fell on the dock banging his head.

"Chris!" He shouted, getting down on his hands and knees.

He hollered his name over and over again.

Chris held onto his throat, he couldn't talk, he couldn't breathe. His eyes were bulging out of their sockets.

He was suffocating, not being able to find the air though it was all around them.

"Help me! Somebody, help me!" Kevin shouted, looking around but no one was there.

There were no boats in the water, there were no people walking by. It was just the two of them.

Kevin began crying as Chris's body began to flop around on the dock like a fish out of water. There was nothing he could do to help him.

He stayed there long after Chris's body stopped moving. Long after Chris had stopped breathing. He knew his friend was dead and it was all his fault.

He was almost asleep next to his friend when he heard his mother calling out to him. He heard Chris's mother too.

"Down here!" He repeated over and over again.

They said when they found him that he was bleeding from his mouth, blood just dripping out, but they couldn't find where he might've cut himself.
He had told them the story, but they didn't believe him.
The doctors called it a seizure, and no one blamed him.
He was just a boy.
But he knew better.
They had taken him to the doctors and even the doctor couldn't find where the blood had been coming from.
Since that day every time that he thought about smiling, he could taste the blood, he thought it was just in his head, but people looked at him and he would wipe his mouth. Blood would be on his shirt, sleeve, or his arm.
It was something that always happened when he thought about smiling and what had happened to Chris.

"It's time for your dental check-up." The nurse came into the room to get him.
He had his private room at the hospital. No one ever came to see him, his parents long dead. It seemed as if everyone had forgotten about him.
"Come on, it can't be that bad. You're the only one in here with real teeth still. Smile, it's not going to kill you." The nurse wheeled him away from the window.
If she only knew.
He tried to smile at the thought and when he did there was a taste of blood.
Warning him.

97

Reminding him that he could never smile again. That's when he felt the blood dripping from his lip and onto his shirt.

Blood droplets to show him that he wasn't crazy for what he thought. Blood to remind him of what happened so long ago.

His smile had killed his best friend. In a sense he was a murderer that had gotten away. He closed his eyes tightly as the blood continued to seep out of his mouth and onto his shirt.

It wasn't until they got to the dentist's office that the dentist's face had grown white. The blood that he'd seen. The teeth that he was looking at when Kevin opened his mouth.

Just a scream and he hit the floor. Dead as a doorknob.

Kevin had smiled in greeting. A test. A theory of his and it was proof that it was him, that it was his smile. The nurse would say it wasn't his fault. Everyone would say that it wasn't, but just like before no one could convince him otherwise.

Not his mother back when he was little and not a therapist that he would go see for the hundredth time that week to explain his theory.

Everyone thought he was crazy. He knew that he wasn't, the dentist lying on the floor was proof that he wasn't insane.

The End

Description

Some thought she was crazy while others thought that she was just a lonely old lady. Day in and day out she sat in the rocking chair knitting away, sometimes they were lucky to hear stories that she told. Everyone knew that the stories she told couldn't be true. Granny wasn't as lonely as everyone thought she was…

Granny

Everyone talked about her as if she wasn't there. The little, old, lady that sat on her porch knitting all the time. Always wearing the same clothes, always with a cigarette hanging out of her mouth.

The ones who visited her would tell how crazy she was.

How she heard voices, the whispers of children that were laughing and playing in the backyard and yet no one was there.

A rusted swing set and that was it. There were no children.

Some say that she might be thinking about her children that had once used the swing set, but she would tell them every day new kids came to play.

Sometimes she would even tell stories of having to beat the children that wouldn't listen. She scared some people away with her soft voice and crazy talk.

Granny would sit in the rocking chair. Rocking back and forth, the creak of the porch going with the rocking.

One evening she got out of her rocker and headed for the backyard. She smiled when she saw the swings moving back and forth.

She made a fire late at night. Her phone ringing inside, she didn't bother to pick it up. She was so slow now that by the time she got in there it would stop ringing.

"Children gather round while I tell you a story." She clapped her hands together.

She watched all the children around the campfire.

They were attentive, their smiles growing wider as she sat on the grass with them. They were all staring at the fire.

"A real one?" A tiny voice asked.

She laughed and nodded her head.

That's when they heard a male's voice coming from the front yard.

"Mother are you back here?" An older gentleman's voice called out.

It was her son. Her only child.

"Yes, you're interrupting right now. Can't you see I'm ready to tell a story?" She asked, looking over her shoulder.

"Mother you need to stop this, no one is there. No one." He shook his head; he knew what the neighbors said.

He could see the way they looked at him when he pulled up in front of the house and he had heard stories of his mother.

She was just a lonely old woman who didn't have anyone to come visit. The only one that did was him.

"Sounds like he needs to be taught a lesson granny. You know what happens when someone interrupts and he's not a very nice man." One of the children nodded their heads.

The smiles off their faces.

Granny nodded her head when the child handed over the sharpened knitting needles. Ones that were meant for such a special occasion.

"What are you doing down there?" He asked her, seeing that she was on the grass.

"Telling a story." She kept the smile on her face, she kept the sweetness in her voice.

He bent down to pick her up. She threw her hands over his neck like she always did when he found her like this.

The children were chanting silently.

"Now. Now. Now." They were growing louder and louder, but she was the only one who could hear them.

She drove the knitting needles into the back of her son's neck. She drove them in so deep that they came out the other side of his throat. He dropped her, trying to speak, his eyes wide.

The only sounds that came from him was gurgling noises. They all watched including Granny as he fell to the ground in front of the fire.

They watched him bleed out.

"He never was one for waiting his turn to speak." Granny's voice was cold, but there was a smile on her face.

The End

Description

She was just a kid. No one listened to kids, even if they were right. What did a kid know? Always telling stories to keep themselves out of trouble. Amber had tried so hard and yet her mother didn't believe her. No one would believe her, not even when it was too late.

Sally.

She had wanted the dolly for so long and she had finally gotten it. It had painted blue eyes, short blonde hair and a pink dress with matching shoes.
She remembered the day she had gotten it and remembered how no one wanted to listen to her.
"Amber, get your doll out of my kitchen. I don't even know how you were able to set it on the counter." Her mother called out.
"I didn't. Sally got up there on her own." Amber tried to tell her, whining at her.
"Don't be silly, dolls can't talk or walk. They are toys." Her mother sighed, rolling her eyes and shaking her head.
Amber took the doll and talked to it as if it were alive, as if it could hear her.
She would put it up with her other dolls and every night she could hear it getting down. She didn't know where it would be in the morning but when she woke up the doll would be gone.
That evening it happened again, only this time it stopped at the foot of Amber's bed.
"Do you want to have fun?" Sally asked.
Amber's eyes grew wide.
"No. It's time for sleep." Amber shook her head, knowing if she got out of bed she would be in trouble.
"Come on, your mother is probably sleeping." Sally giggled and ran for the bedroom door that was always open just ajar so that Amber could have the light like she needed.

Amber got out of bed, not because she wanted to but because she wanted to see what Sally was up to.

It was the first time that she'd ever heard Sally talk to her.

She wished that she could go to her mother, but she wouldn't believe her.

No one would.

Sally ran around the house giggling and wound up in Amber's mother's room.

"What are you doing?" Amber asked in a hushed voice.

"We can play doctor." Sally climbed up on the bed and grabbed the scissors from the nightstand.

"No." Amber almost shouted.

She felt the fear; she felt the tears coming to her eyes. The way Sally had said it sounded scary; it wouldn't be the first time that Sally had done something dangerous.

Sally took the scissors and Amber was looking for something that she could capture Sally in.

There was a long chest in the bedroom. All she had to do was get it open.

Keeping an eye on Sally who was getting closer and closer to her mother with the pointed scissors she flung the chest open.

Sally had her arm up in the air, ready to jab them into her mother's throat when Amber grabbed her from behind.

Sally shouted and bit. She dropped the scissors and Amber threw her into the chest. Slamming the chest down.

She felt the painful bite on her arm.

"Amber, what are you doing in here?" She asked, waking up to Sally's shouts from the chest.

"You need to help me." Amber began crying.

"What is going on?" She flung the covers off her and walked over to Amber who was fighting to keep the chest closed.

"Who do you have in there?" Her mother glared down at her.

"Sally is trying to come out. She's trying to get out!" Amber cried out, the tears coming to her eyes.

"Sally can't come alive!" Her mother was getting upset that Amber blamed everything on Sally.

A doll that couldn't do any harm to anyone.

"You just don't want to stay in bed." Her mother sighed, taking Amber off the chest.

The only explanation was that Amber had a friend over and they were playing a game. Though she didn't recall Amber inviting a friend over.

When she opened the chest, Sally sprang out with a broken piece of a picture frame. The second Amber's mother started screaming she knew it was over.

She had tried to tell her; she didn't want to listen. Her mother's screams got louder and louder and Amber covered her ears tightly as she ran from the room.

As she ran from the house.

It wouldn't be long until the police were called, and she would tell them the story. She would tell them like she'd told them a hundred times before and once again they wouldn't listen to her…

Description.

She thought that she could trust him. She had known him for years and yet, now she was running from him, her parents were gone. Running through the woods she could hear his heavy breathing behind her. She knew that he was giving chase. Thinking there was no one who could help her she came across a shack in the middle of the woods. Lights were on. There was a shimmer of hope when she saw the shack. That is until she realized what the shack was for and there was no way to escape what she had seen. She couldn't erase the images from her mind…

Captured.

She had been running, escaping the man that had killed her mother and father. Trying to run from the man that would always find her.
Her heart was racing as she ran through the woods. Her feet hurt, running barefoot through the woods was easier than running in shoes.
They were miles away from everyone. It was what he had wanted. No one that she could talk to, no one that she could turn to.
It was hard to see where she was running, her eyes were blurred with tears that were filling her eyes and spilling down her face.
It's when she saw the light. She felt a smile come to her face.
A shack of sorts and someone had to live there if there was a light on.
There just had to be someone who could help her.
She banged on the shack door when she reached it, she looked over her shoulder she didn't believe that he was giving chase anymore.
There was no answer at the door, she tried the knob and it turned easily as she pushed against the door.
She was in the shack. She was safe. At least that's what she thought. Locking the door, she pressed her back against it.
That's when her eyes came into focus.
Lining the walls of the shack were jars filled with a clear liquid. The closer she got to them, the more she realized they were human eyes!

Eyes that were crystal blue. The prettiest blue that she'd ever seen.

She covered her mouth to keep herself from screaming.

Her legs were all scratched up from the branches and twigs that she had run through.

She walked around the shack and saw that on another shelf there were tongues. Tongues that had been cut out of human-beings and she stuck her own tongue out to match it with the ones that she was seeing.

A pounding on the door made her jump!

"I know you're in there. Give me what I want." He growled through the door.

His fists beating on the door. It was a thin door. An old door, she knew soon he would break through it. She was looking for an escape and there was none. Just four walls. The only exit was the door she had walked into.

She began crying again when the door was busted down.

"How could you do this?" She shook her head back and forth.

He had a knife in his hand, and she knew what he was going to do.

"You thought that you knew me. We've been married for years, never once had you asked where I was going." He laughed.

Taking her by the nape of her neck he head-butted her as hard as he could.

She tried to stay coherent. Tried to stay focused on him.

Her eyes lost focus and she saw nothing but darkness. She had lost.

It took him hours, but he had finally managed to do it. A new set of blue eyes that would only turn bluer. Another fresh tongue that would never shrivel even long after he was gone.

The End

Description.

She was an adult now and thought she could never be convinced that her imagination was running wild. One story, one disappearance that had never been believed as a child. It was just a story, a made-up story to give kids a good scare. Something that wasn't meant to stay lodged in the memory. For her it had been there since she heard the story. She hoped it was a blessing in disguise…

Hiding.

"What are you doing in the dark?" The doctor asked her.
"Hiding." Lilly whispered.
"In the corner? Who are you hiding from?" He asked her.
They'd been through this a hundred times before. She was a woman of thirty-two who still believed the story of the boogeyman since she was a child. Since the first time that she had ever heard the story she thought it to be true.
"Not who, what." She closed her eyes she knew she was safe.
She was safe in the corner and she was safe in the dark.
There was only one place that the boogeyman lived and that was under the bed.
"It's not real. It's your imagination telling you it's real. You know why we are here tonight, right?" The doctor asked her.
He was writing something down on the pad of paper that he kept beside him.
"Yes." The fear in her voice was showing.
"Why are we here?" He asked her, wanting her to put it into her own words.
"That bed is where you want me to sleep. You are going to watch me while I sleep behind that thick mirror on the wall." She nodded her head.
"That's right. To prove to you there's no such thing as the boogeyman." He finished for her, giving her a smile.

The smile was supposed to be soothing, but it only scared her more.

She had signed up for this, now that the time was here, she wasn't sure that she could do it.

"We can leave a light on." He suggested.

"No, that won't help. It will only help him." She shook her head back and forth.

The doctor got up out of his chair and made his way to her in the dark. He took her hand and helped her out of the corner.

She moved willingly.

Like a child he helped her to the bed in the middle of the room. He tucked her in and gave her a smile.

"I'm going to be just in the next room. I will show you, in the morning you will see." His whispered voice held a promise that she knew he wasn't going to be able to fulfill.

Maybe it would be better this way. Maybe showing someone else, someone would believe her. That there was a boogeyman.

It wasn't just a story. She had seen it before, when she was younger. It had taken her friend during a sleepover.

People were looking for her and she knew that her friend would never be found. Once the boogeyman took you, that was it.

You would never again see the light of day.

She covered herself all the way to her chin, watched the doctor leave the room and saw the light turn on where the mirror was.

He waved at her; she didn't wave back. There was no smile upon her face.

It didn't take long before the medication made her tired.
She tried hard to keep her eyes open, but she had lost the fight to sleep.
The doctor watched her throughout the night.
He couldn't wait to get through this with her, it had been years since he could convince her to do this and now that it was happening, he couldn't wait to prove to her that nothing was there. That there was no such thing as the boogeyman. Just a tale to tell kids around a campfire or when there was a sleepover at someone's house down in the living room.
He remembered the story and he had laughed it off when he was a child. Just like any normal child it was soon forgotten within a day or so.
That's when he heard the noise.
The clattering around.
That's when he saw the black beast, crawling out from under the bed. Going for her. She was sleeping peacefully.
He quickly let the other room and slammed the door open in the room where she was.
"Let her go! Let her go!" The doctor was shouting and hollering.
He knew that no one was coming for help.
He had sent everyone home in hopes that he could get her to stay if it was just the two of them. She trusted him, had gone to him for years.
All this time he couldn't believe how right she had been! He hadn't listened when he should've, chalking her up to having a nightmare and her friend truly just disappeared.

The boogeyman had red eyes, a black, scaly body. It had a snout like a dragon and the ears of a wolf.
The boogeyman grabbed her and quickly left with her.
The doctor raced to the bed.
Looking under it there was nothing. No signs that she had been there at all. No signs that the boogeyman had entered the room and left.
He was all the way under the bed and found nothing. As soon as he tried slipping out, he had almost made it out from under the bed when he felt something grab his wrist.
He tried pulling away, the grip got tighter, the strength got stronger.
Within seconds the room was empty. It would be empty until the next day.
No one would know what happened to her.
Or what happened to the doctor.
The tape played on through the night. However, the tape would only be blank when it was played over and over again.
A story would be created of how the two could just disappear, vanish into thin air. Stories that would haunt the hospital forever.

The End

Description

She couldn't hear anything — nothing from the other side.

"Help me!" She shouted, trying to pull her head back through the mirror.

Realizing she couldn't, she felt her heart beating quickly. She felt her eyes growing wider.

It was too dark she couldn't see anything.

"You've come to play with us, Alicia. You have heard us." The voice was soft and low. It was hot, not just hot like breath, but hot like fire.

"I want to go home." She swallowed the lump in her throat.

She was sweating.

"We don't go home here."

With that, she felt herself being pulled further into the mirror. There was no stopping the pull though she tried to fight it.

Carnival.

The mirrors were amazing, one of the things that Alicia liked. The mirrors when it came to carnivals. Showing how skinny she was or how short she was. How thin she was or how fat she was. Her nose was bigger than her eyes when she moved in close, and her eyes were little, tiny, dots when she moved further away.

Even at fifteen years old, she was still amazed by them.

As she began to leave, she heard something. It sounded like someone whispering her name.

Alicia looked at the mirror that she was about to leave.

Alicia, come play.

The words were repeated again and again.

She giggled wondering if it was some kind of joke that her friends were playing on her. A trick maybe.

She pressed her face against the mirror and found her head going through it.

She screamed but no one could hear her on this side. Didn't anyone see anything that was going on? Didn't anyone think that it was weird that her head was stuck in the mirror?

She couldn't hear anything — nothing from the other side.

"Help me!" She shouted, trying to pull her head back through the mirror.

Realizing she couldn't, she felt her heart beating quickly. She felt her eyes growing wider.

It was too dark she couldn't see anything.

"You've come to play with us, Alicia. You have heard us." The voice was soft and low. It was hot, not just hot like breath, but hot like fire.

"I want to go home." She swallowed the lump in her throat.

She was sweating.

"We don't go home here."

With that, she felt herself being pulled further into the mirror. There was no stopping the pull though she tried to fight it.

She saw a light, a small light coming towards her. Soon it was so bright that she had to shield her eyes. There were skeletons dancing around; they were holding hands in a circle. Dancing to the music she couldn't hear.

It was then that she realized that all of them had been young.

"I want to go home!" She screamed.

But they weren't listening. Turning around the mirror was gone. The room began to heat up. She was getting hotter and hotter.

"No one gets to leave here." The skeletons sang louder and louder.

They sang it so much that she had to cover her ears. Shaking her head back and forth.

She realized how they had become skeletons so quickly.

They had melted.

Alicia took her hands away from her ears when she realized that her arms were melting. Her skin was melting!

It didn't hurt, she didn't feel an ounce of pain, but the shock of it all. She couldn't believe that it was real.

She refused to believe that it would be real. That it could be.

"NO!" She screamed at the top of her lungs.

It was then that she fell.

She bumped her head, and it took her a few minutes to realize where she was.

In her own room, the sun shining, her alarm going off.

Breathing in and out, wiping the sweat off her face, she realized it had all been a dream. Just a horrible dream.

She laughed at herself for acting so silly.

It had seemed so real to her everything had been real behind the mirror.

Alicia was still shaking when she got on her feet.

"Come on. It was just a dream." She muttered to herself as she shut the alarm off.

There was a knock on the door.

"Come in." Alicia called out.

"Are you ready? Are you ready to go to the carnival? I know how much you love the mirrors." Her friend laughed as she made her way into the room.

Alicia's smile faded from her face.

There was no way that she was going to go anywhere near the mirrors. The dream was enough to make her realize that not everything was as it seemed.

"Maybe not the mirrors but we can definitely go on the rides." Alicia grinned.

There would be no mirrors for her anymore. Not when it came to the carnival at least.

"Okay, since when do you not like the mirrors?" Her friend pounced on her bed.

"Since now. I think we're getting a little too old for the mirrors." Alicia shrugged her shoulders like it was no big deal.
She wasn't going to tell anyone about her dream.
Everyone would think she was crazy.
Such a big warning and just in the nick of time. She didn't even want to wonder if her dream would come true. She didn't want to take the chance that maybe she wasn't crazy.
"Since we are skipping the mirrors. You have to go on whatever ride I want." Her friend hugged her tight around the neck.
"Sounds good to me." Alicia smiled.
Just as long as it wasn't mirrors.

The End.

Description

"Don't go!" The woman called out her warning.
Sadie didn't look back; she left the tent. There was no way that she was going to listen to someone who didn't even know her.
The woman didn't even take her money, didn't even ask for it.
In the middle of the woods, pitch black, even the moon wasn't shining.
"Crazy, old, woman." Sadie shook her head back and forth.
Sadie did go back though she wasn't going to leave the old woman without any money at all. Though her fortune was wrong.
Sadie had only gone a short distance.
There was nothing there.
The tent was gone as if it had vanished into thin air.
"Hey!" Sadie shouted, looking around.
She couldn't be going crazy and yet there was no sign of the woman.
"I forgot to pay you!" Sadie shouted into the dark.
The woman didn't appear, neither did the tent.
Sadie sighed heavily and headed back the way she came.

Fortuneteller

It was her first time going. Her brother had convinced her to go and now she was sitting in front of a creepy, old, lady who looked more like a gypsy. She looked into the globe of which the fortuneteller could tell her future.

There was no smile on her face.

"You're in grave danger." The woman's brown eyes that were sunken in looked up from her crystal ball.

Sadie didn't say anything. She didn't know what to say. She couldn't tell the woman that she was full of it.

"What do you mean?" She finally asked, seeing that the old woman wasn't smiling at all.

"There is no future for you." The fortuneteller shook her head, backing away from the table. It looked as if the old woman was scared.

"I don't understand." Sadie felt her heart racing.

"Having no future means that you're not going to be here. A horrible fate. Death." The old woman shook her head back and forth.

Sadie didn't want to hear anymore.

Death?

Her brother made her come here for this.

"You're crazy. I told my brother you were." Sadie pushed her chair back away from the table.

"Don't go!" The woman called out her warning.

Sadie didn't look, back she left the tent. There was no way that she was going to listen to someone who didn't even know her.

The woman didn't even take her money, didn't even ask for it.

In the middle of the woods, pitch black, even the moon wasn't shining.

"Crazy, old, woman." Sadie shook her head back and forth.

Sadie did go back, though she wasn't going to leave the old woman without any money at all. Though her fortune was wrong.

Sadie had only gone a short distance.

There was nothing there.

The tent was gone as if it had vanished into thin air.

"Hey!" Sadie shouted, looking around.

She couldn't be going crazy and yet there was no sign of the woman.

"I forgot to pay you!" Sadie shouted into the dark.

The woman didn't appear, neither did the tent.

Sadie sighed heavily and headed back the way she came.

Who didn't want their money? Who didn't want to be paid even though it was a con job? She didn't know but if the woman was nowhere to be found she wasn't going to track her down.

"No future. I'm living it right now." Sadie muttered, realizing just how crazy the woman was.

She was just about out of the woods when she heard rustling behind her.

Sadie stopped for just a moment and maybe she shouldn't have. But she did.

Turning slowly to see what was behind her, she wasn't one fearing the dark. Never had she worried about anything swallowing her up.

When she turned, she saw a black creature she couldn't quite make it out. She knew it was big, it had red eyes.

She tried to scream as the thing lunged at her.

On the ground Sadie struggled underneath the hairy beast.

She felt it biting into her, eating her flesh as she stared up at the dark sky.

There was no way for her to scream, the pain that she felt. No one could hear her it was as if her voice box was gone.

"You didn't want to believe me. You thought that I was crazy. I told you not to leave the tent. You didn't listen. If you had listened, I might have been able to save you." The old woman's voice came.

Sadie wasn't sure if she was hearing things, but if she wasn't, the voice was coming from the creature itself.

"I am not crazy, neither are you. No one wants to believe me. I am trapped in that tent. I am trapped for all eternity until someone listens to me. You're not the first. I am the beast in the night. The one who sees what your future will be like." The creature's mind was telling her.

Sadie closed her eyes tightly she felt the blood draining from her body. The dead leaves of fall under her though she couldn't move.

The last thing that she saw before her eyes glazed over was the tent.

It had reappeared.

The creature was now the old woman.

The woman that she had thought was crazy.

"All you had to do was listen to me. I tried to warn you. You ran, you thought that I was crazy. Not

knowing what I was talking about. The creature, it's inside of me. I am its slave and you will not be the last one that it comes for. You will not be the last one that runs from my tent." The old woman whispered.
That was the last thing that Sadie heard.
The last thing she saw wasn't the creature itself but the old woman that had tried to help her. That wanted to help her.
Sadie's mind was shutting down. How could she have come into these woods? Why did her brother send her? Did he know?
It was something that Sadie would never find out. Though she was sure he'd come looking for her, she had a feeling that she would never be found.
Just like the tent, how it had disappeared. She was sure that's what would happen to her body.
It would just disappear.
"I tried, I tried so hard to keep you safe. The second you left the tent I knew what was going to happen. I couldn't save you. I can't save anyone who isn't willing to listen. I'm so sorry that it's ended this way." The old woman turned back into the creature and devoured her.
They wouldn't even find Sadie's bones. Not a trace of her no matter how hard they tried to, she had become a mystery in the night. One that they would never solve no matter how hard they tried.
A missing teen that they would search for but would never find. One that they thought had become a runaway after a few years of crying and searching.

The End

Description

"Come on, it's all in fun. What's the matter Allan, you don't like fun?" Cory asked him, teasing him.
Allan didn't answer him.
Night came faster than he thought it would. Soon he was tied to a tree trunk. His hands behind the tree tied so tightly he could feel his hands going to sleep.
They all left. Every single one of them.
Allan wasn't scared. The moon was full, the light of it shined down on him.
That's when he heard the rustling of the dead leaves. The low growl that was getting closer and closer to him!
"Alright guys, very funny." Allan called out.
No one answered him.
The growl grew deeper, it was closer than the last time.
Allan began tugging on the rope that held his wrists. He couldn't move them.
"Cory, come on!" Allan shouted out this time.
He didn't care if everyone laughed at him now. He didn't care if they teased him, he just wanted out of the woods.

Dare You.

Allan wasn't one for turning down any dare. Not from his friends and not from his siblings. A new kid had come to town, wanted to be part of the group. Allan didn't like him from the start, his friends did though.
"I dare you to sleep outback of my house." The new kid Cory grinned at Allan.
He had heard all about Allan. How he would take dares no matter what it was.
"That's not even a dare." Allan rolled his eyes.
His friends laughed.
"You haven't heard the rest of it." Cory grinned.
They waited for him to finish. All eyes on Cory who wanted to be the big shot. That's why Allan didn't like him.
"You have to be tied to a tree in the middle of the woods. Tonight's the full moon." Cory pointed a finger at him.
Alan could already see the sun was setting. He wasn't supposed to be home anyways. Spending the night at one of his friend's houses had been okayed.
"There's nothing scary about the full moon. Nothing scary about being tied up to a tree." Allan threw his head back and laughed.
"Will you do it?" Cory asked him.
"No. I don't take dares that are that simple." Allan didn't even think about it.
"Is Allan Dunbar turning down the first dare of his life?" One of his friends clapped him on the shoulder and teased him.
The kids laughed at him, including Cory.

It was as if Cory had this planned. At least that's what Allan thought.

"Fine, fine. I will take the stupid dare. I'm not going to turn down the dare." Allan rolled his eyes. He didn't like the fact that his friends were all laughing at him.

"Tonight, at midnight I dare you to stay in the woods tied to a tree." Cory knew how to start the challenge.

"Challenge accepted." Allan didn't hesitate this time. His pride in the way, his feelings hurt that his friends would sit there and laugh at him.

"We are all going to make sure that you are tied properly to the tree." Cory looked at the group and they all nodded their heads.

"Since when does Cory get to make all the decisions?" Allan glared at his friends, he had enough of Cory playing boss.

"Come on, it's all in fun. What's the matter Allan, you don't like fun?" Cory asked him, teasing him.

Allan didn't answer him.

Night came faster than he thought it would. Soon he was tied to a tree trunk. His hands behind the tree tied so tightly he could feel his hands going to sleep.

They all left. Every single one of them.

Allan wasn't scared. The moon was full, the light of it shined down on him.

That's when he heard the rustling of the dead leaves.

The low growl that was getting closer and closer to him!

"Alright guys, very funny." Allan called out.

No one answered him.

The growl grew deeper, it was closer than the last time.

Allan began tugging on the rope that held his wrists. He couldn't move them.

"Cory, come on!" Allan shouted out this time.

He didn't care if everyone laughed at him now. He didn't care if they teased him, he just wanted out of the woods.

That's when he saw it. The creature was on all fours. Though something was familiar about the creature with its sharp teeth, drool coming off the creature's mouth!

"Cory!" Allan shouted, he blinked twice trying to understand it.

"The creature in the night needs to feed." The voice came back, Cory's voice!

His eyes turned green. The fur was a raggedy black, the tips on end as the creature came closer and closer. Allan wanted to scream, he kicked out and the creature snapped at his feet with its jowl's snapping. Allan could hear its teeth clanging together.

Just as Allan was about to press his head back against the tree and let out a rippling scream the creature pounced.

Everything was dark, he could feel the sharp teeth around his throat. In one quick motion Allan's body went lip.

The creature pulled away from Allan chewing and snorting angrily.

It sniffed around Allan's headless body and quickly formed back into Cory.

His mouth covered in Allan's blood, it was a bitter yet sweet taste on his tongue as he slowly went into his house, entering through the back door to head upstairs and take a shower.

The beast was full for now. It wouldn't be long before he would feast again though. Cory laughed as he let the shower water run down the back of his neck.

The End

Description

"The mess monster doesn't come out until bedtime. It rattles around, playing with whatever mess you left under your bed. Slowly it creeps out and slithers into your blanket. It doesn't matter how tightly you bundle yourself up. The mess monster always finds a way to get to you. When it does, when it finally has you, it brings you under the bed. Fight and yell as loud as you might but no one will ever hear you. Forever gone with the mess that you've left. Your own mess takes you under the bed. Never to be seen again." He told the story in a whispered voice his eyes were the only thing that showed from the flashlight that he was holding.

It's Not Real

That's what he had tried to tell himself. It was his first sleepover, and he had to convince himself that all he was seeing under the bed were the light up shoes that his parents had bought him.

At ten years old he wasn't scared of anything. Well, maybe one thing.

What was under the bed.

Though in the daylight there was nothing but toys, his shoes, and some coloring books. His mother had always told him to clean out from under his bed or the mess monster would come out and grab him.

Just a joke. He knew that.

When night fell through, he didn't dare look under his bed. He didn't want to see the mess monster he even had his mother leave the hall light on.

When asked why he wouldn't give her a reason, but she left it on just the same.

They were in his room that night. They were sitting around in a circle on the floor. He couldn't help but look under his bed.

"What is the matter with you? Are you afraid of the boogeyman?" His friend Tyler asked.

"No, there's no such thing." He glared.

Wishing they would turn on the lights instead of using the flashlights.

His bedroom door was closed.

That never happened.

"I know there isn't, but you should see your eyes." Tyler laughed and pointed at him.

It was as if he was the butt of Tyler's jokes.

"There is such a thing as the mess monster though." He didn't know what else to say as he gave an eerie laugh of his own.

He put his face into the beam of the flashlight to make himself look scary.

"You know there isn't. Cut the shit." Tyler pushed him lightly.

The other boys laughed.

It was all fun and games.

"Do you want to hear the story of the mess monster or not?" He asked Tyler, raising his eyebrows though his heart was beating hard against his chest.

He could feel the sweat coming to his face.

"Yeah, let's hear it." Tyler nodded his head, the tight smirk on his face.

"The mess monster doesn't come out until bedtime. It rattles around, playing with whatever mess you left under your bed. Slowly it creeps out and slithers into your blanket. It doesn't matter how tightly you bundle yourself up. The mess monster always finds a way to get to you. When it does, when it finally has you, it brings you under the bed. Fight and yell as loud as you might but no one will ever hear you. Forever gone with the mess that you've left. Your own mess takes you under the bed. Never to be seen again." He told the story in a whispered voice his eyes were the only thing that showed from the flashlight that he was holding.

It was eerily quiet and one of their friends lightly tapped Tyler on the shoulder. He jumped, his own heart racing.

"That's not true. There is no such thing as monsters." Tyler glared at their friend. Tyler glared at him.

"Then why are you scared?" He asked.

"I'm not." Tyler grumbled.

"No?" He asked.

"No." Tyler stated firmly.

"Look under my bed. There's a mess under there." He laughed, challenging him.

Tyler turned and looked under the bed from where he was.

"No, look closer." He sighed, shaking his head back and forth.

Tyler crawled over to it and shoved his hand under with a smile on his face. He looked at the group of boys.

"I told you there's no such thing as-" His voice was cut off.

They watched as he was being dragged under the bed. They tried to help Tyler. Tried to pull him back towards the group. They grabbed his legs, his hips but the force was much stronger than he was.

Before they knew it, Tyler was gone! There was no way to help him. All the boys looked under the bed. Tyler had disappeared and the mess that had been made. There was nothing under his bed. Not even his light up shoes that had scared him last night.

They all looked at him.

"It was just a story, I made up the story. It wasn't real!" He shook his head, backing away from them. He didn't know how he was going to explain. No one was going to believe him.

"This we keep to ourselves. Tyler was never here." One of the boys whispered, not wanting to get into trouble for something that wasn't believable.

That night the boys made a pact. That Tyler had never shown up. It was a secret that they would remember for years to come and take to the grave with them. Now that he realized the mess monster was real, he made sure not even to leave his shoes under the bed. As a grown man his wife laughed at him, teased him about it, but if she had only been there that night she wouldn't have.

The End

Description.

"What happened to Jamie. I want to know." Lindsey stood in the doorway.
"Swamp water." Her mother shrugged her shoulders, she didn't even look at her.
"I'm old enough to know what happened to her." Lindsey wasn't going to take that for an answer anymore.
"Jamie is gone, she's not coming back." Her father thought that he had put an end to it.
Thought that was all that would become of it.
"I'm going to the swamp." Lindsey tested her theory.
"No!" Her mother shouted, getting up from the chair. Her eyes were filling with tears. She was scared, Lindsey could see that. Her body was shaking. Her mother hadn't been lying to her.
Whatever happened to Jamie happened in the swamp.

What Happened to Jamie?

That's what she wanted to know. She wanted to know what happened to her best friend Jamie, why was it that she wasn't here? They hadn't found her; it had been almost two years since she had seen her. Everyone thought she had just moved away but Lindsey knew better. Her parents cried the day they couldn't find her.

Whenever she asked her parents, they would just say swamp water and shake their heads. They were still sad. Just as sad as she was herself.

It was Lindsey's sixteenth birthday and it was getting harder for her. They did everything together.

She didn't want a birthday without Jamie.

Lindsey thought long and hard as she sat that evening. Her birthday almost over and done with until next year.

Why would they only say swamp water? The only swamp that was around was a few blocks away. Jamie would never go there.

"They're crazy." Lindsey whispered, shaking her head and going into the house.

Her parents were watching television.

"What happened to Jamie. I want to know." Lindsey stood in the doorway.

"Swamp water." Her mother shrugged her shoulders, she didn't even look at her.

"I'm old enough to know what happened to her." Lindsey wasn't going to take that for an answer anymore.

"Jamie is gone, she's not coming back." Her father thought that he had put an end to it.

Thought that was all that would become of it.

"I'm going to the swamp." Lindsey tested her theory.

"No!" Her mother shouted, getting up from the chair. Her eyes were filling with tears. She was scared, Lindsey could see that. Her body was shaking. Her mother hadn't been lying to her.

Whatever happened to Jamie happened in the swamp.

"Okay, okay, I won't." Lindsey whispered, hugging her mother tightly to her.

She went upstairs to go to bed. Waiting for her parents to go to bed.

Lindsey packed a few things in a bag and snuck out her window. Her window led out onto a roof that dipped down so it was close enough to jump to the ground without getting hurt.

Lindsey hurried to the swamp. It was foggy as she shined her flashlight down at the ground to see where she was going.

Her heart was racing as she sat down at the edge of the swamp.

"Jamie, please, where are you?" Lindsey whispered into the swamp.

The bubbles came then, her eyes grew wide as she pushed herself away from the edge.

Jamie!

"Go back, go back home before you become like me!" Jamie was covered in moss, covered in slimy filth from the bottom of the swamp.

"How, how did you get here?" Lindsey wasn't going to show her that she was afraid. She could never be afraid of her best friend.

"They put me here. You'd better go before they put you here too. They sacrificed me." Jamie's voice was gargling.

It was as if she had swallowed a lot of water.

"Who Jamie, please tell me who." Lindsey felt the tears coming to her eyes.

Jamie shook her head and slowly began to go back into the swamp.

It was then that Lindsey felt the hands climbing up her feet. There were numerous hands coming out of the swamp and she could feel herself being tugged closer and closer.

"I tried to tell you. I tried to make you go back." That was the last time she had seen Jamie. Their eyes met. Lindsey could see the sorrow in them as she was being pulled closer and closer to the swamp. She tried to push them away, she tried to claw her way back onto the edge.

They were too strong.

Monsters of the swamp.

That's when it dawned on her.

The stories to scare each other, the stories to scare the neighborhood kids to keep them away from the swamp. To make sure that they didn't go there and end up disappearing.

The swamp monsters weren't fake, they were real! Their parents trying to keep them away, trying to warn them and there was nothing that anyone could do now.

Lindsey felt her heart pounding, she felt her eyes growing wider and wider as her body was being dragged further and further into the cold, swampy, water.

There was no escaping.
She couldn't escape the dark night, she couldn't escape the cold, clammy hands that were dragging down deeper and deeper into the swamp.
There was just no way around it.
It wasn't until she hit the bottom that she could see through the swampy muck. Jamie was there. She was holding her hand.
"Soon it won't hurt anymore. Soon we will have more friends down here. No one ever stays away from the swamp water. They are too brave, they are nosey."
Jamie's voice was nothing more than a whisper.
Lindsey closed her eyes, the swamp water filling her lungs and she knew then that her mother was trying to keep her safe.
The look that was on her face that evening. Now it would stay there forever. Her parents would move away just like Jamie's had to forget the horror. To forget the pain. Maybe to forget Lindsey altogether…

The End

Description

The stars were out, the moon was high in the sky now. The air warm, the water cold.

"We tell no one Kendra. Do you hear me?" Susan asked.

She had gotten so close to Kendra her voice was so cold that Kendra saw the words more as a threat than anything else.

She found herself nodding her head.

"We go home, and we tell no one." Susan jabbed a finger against her chest.

"I'm supposed to sleep over tonight. Samantha was supposed to…" She let her voice trail off and looked over her shoulder at the dark water.

SAMANTHA

It was a day of fun in the sun and swimming. At least that's how it started out. Kendra, Susan and Samantha went swimming all day. The sun was setting when they were making their way back to shore. They had gone out further than what Samantha had realized. Her arms were tired, her legs were tired.
"Guys, I don't know if I can make it back." Samantha was beginning to panic.
"You can, come on." Kendra looked over her shoulder.
She didn't realize how much Samantha was struggling then. Susan was too far ahead to hear either of them.
That was until she heard a scream.
Susan stopped swimming, treading water she turned around and saw that Samantha was slowly going under.
She felt her heart race.
Swimming back towards Kendra and Samantha she could see that Kendra was doing all that she could to get to Samantha.
"Help me!" Samantha began crying, spitting up the water that had entered her mouth. Her last cries for help.
Her head went under, her fingertips had vanished before the girls could get to her. They looked at one another and went under the water to look for her.
All three of them were great swimmers.

They looked through the water the best they could. It was night, they couldn't see anything. When they came up for air, they could still hear her screams.

"Samantha! We hear you, where are you!?" Kendra shouted back.

The only thing that came back to her was her own echo.

They searched and searched the waters, looking for her. There was no sign of her.

"We need to go for help." Kendra looked at Susan.

Susan was the one who shook her head as she headed back towards the shore. She could hear Kendra swimming after her.

"We need to tell someone, Susan!" Kendra shouted when she felt her feet hit the sand.

"We can't tell anyone! They are going to blame it on us! You know that!" Susan shouted back, tears coming out of her eyes and sliding down her face.

"Then what are we supposed to do? Pretend that it never happened?" Kendra moved her wet hair from her face.

"I don't know, no one is going to believe that we couldn't find her. No one is going to believe that we tried to help her." Susan lowered her voice.

The stars were out, the moon was high in the sky now. The air warm, the water cold.

"We tell no one Kendra. Do you hear me?" Susan asked.

She had gotten so close to Kendra her voice was so cold that Kendra saw the words more as a threat than anything else.

She found herself nodding her head.

"We go home, and we tell no one." Susan jabbed a finger against her chest.

"I'm supposed to sleep over tonight. Samantha was supposed to…" She let her voice trail off and looked over her shoulder at the dark water.

It looked so inviting earlier, now it looked as if it was calling to them. The water hoping to grab them as it had Samantha.

"We don't know where she went. If anyone asks, she said she'd meet us back at my house, but she never showed up." Susan had thought of a story quick.

"It's not the right thing to do. You know that." Kendra whispered.

"Do you want to get into trouble? Is that what you want? I'm not talking about being grounded either." Susan filled her head with the things she hadn't said.

Kendra shook her head back and forth slowly.

That night as they were laying under the covers they didn't talk, they couldn't even sleep. The last words were of Samantha begging for help and they had covered it up. They swam away and here they were.

That's when they heard the noise.

It started in the hall. They heard the wet footsteps on the hardwood floor and looked at one another in the dark.

Susan shook her head back and forth as Kendra began to whimper.

The wet footsteps were coming closer and closer to the open bedroom door.

They stared at the door, their eyes growing wider and wider.

They saw the shadow before they saw the body.

"I asked. I pleaded." The watery voice came before she stood in the doorway.

Her hair was scraggly, her lips were blue. Her eyes black as coal as she stood there staring at the two.

"We tried." Kendra whimpered, huddling closer to Susan.

"You let me die. You left me there." Samantha's fingers were shaking, her body was shaking as she continued to enter the room.

"You're dead." Susan whispered.

"Sometimes the dead come back for the ones who deserve it." Samantha touched them she was cold as ice.

"Now you're dead too." Samantha whispered against Susan's ear.

Samantha's watery voice was the last thing that either of the girls had heard before their bodies began to turn ice cold. Teeth chattering, eyes wide.

Samantha laughed and laughed, feeling the water rushing through her body, making them feel everything that she had to feel.

No one should keep a tragedy so close to them. No one should keep secrets, that was how Samantha had felt.

The End

Description

They were best friends. Adam had convinced him to go out back to the tracks. They were playing on them. Pushing each other, they were playing chicken.
He had told Jason that he was always scared of everything. That they never had any fun. Told Jason that if he didn't play, they weren't going to be friends anymore.
Jason believed him.
Jason was out to prove to his friend that he wasn't scared. That he could play games just like anyone else could.
The train was getting closer and closer as they jumped on the tracks and jumped off quickly.
Knowing that they weren't going to get hit.
Adam had begged for Jason not to do it again.
Begged and still Jason laughed at him.
Jason was going to prove his point.

Whistling Train

Calvin couldn't keep the words out of his head. He had lived with it all his life. Rocking back and forth in the rocking chair as he watched the fight on television at sixty-five years old, he couldn't help but wonder what if?

If he had been there that day, his brother wouldn't be dead. He would probably be talking to him on the phone right now.

But he hadn't been there. He'd been out with his girlfriend. He was supposed to be watching his brother that night. He thought the football game and spending time with his girlfriend was more important. He had waited for his brother to go to sleep that night before he even left the house…

He looked in on Jason. He knew that he was sleeping. Calvin knew he would be home hours before his parents came home. At seventeen the only thing he cared about was going to the games, girls, and hanging out with his buddies. They had already told him his plans were cancelled when he came home from school. That's what they thought.

He smiled as he closed Jason's bedroom door and headed out when he heard a honk in the driveway. Quickly he raced out of the house and shook his head, he didn't want the noise waking up his little brother. Little really wasn't the word. Jason had been thirteen. Old enough to stay at home by himself. He was still a kid though. Scared of his own shadow.

He wasn't sure why Jason had even left the house that night himself. A question that would never be answered.

When he got home that night, there were cops and an ambulance. There were his parents crying and looking at him as if he'd done something that was unforgivable.

A stretcher came out from the back yard. He could see his brother. The blood soaking the stretcher. The sheet covered him, but it slipped down a little when they hoisted him into the ambulance.

What had happened was the midnight train came through occasionally in the back. There were train tracks when the ambulance was gone Calvin got a little closer and noticed a boy about Jason's age. He remembered the kid. Adam.

They were best friends. Adam had convinced him to go out back to the tracks. They were playing on them. Pushing each other, they were playing chicken.

He had told Jason that he was always scared of everything. That they never had any fun. Told Jason that if he didn't play, they weren't going to be friends anymore.

Jason believed him.

Jason was out to prove to his friend that he wasn't scared. That he could play games just like anyone else could.

The train was getting closer and closer as they jumped on the tracks and jumped off quickly. Knowing that they weren't going to get hit. Adam had begged for Jason not to do it again. Begged and still Jason laughed at him. Jason was going to prove his point.

He jumped one more time, there was enough time to get off the track. Enough time for Jason to move but he couldn't.
The terror in his eyes Adam had recalled was like no other.
"My shoelace!" Jason shouted.
Those were the last words that had come from his mouth before the train hit him.
His shoelace had gotten stuck under the wood. He didn't have time to take it off.
Adam told the story with tears in his eyes. He was sorry for what had happened. Seeing the look on Adam's face. Then seeing the look on his parent's face. They blamed him, all of them did though they didn't come out and say it.
Calvin could feel it, up until his parents died.
They would never come out and say that he was the reason Jason was dead. But it was. He even knew it was.

Calvin continued to rock in his rocking chair. He shut the television off and listened to the silence for just a minute, it was nice and quiet. So quiet that he could hear the clock ticking on the wall.
Then he heard it.
The whistle of the train. He listened even closer as the train got closer and closer. He heard a boy's laughter. Jason's laughter.
He always listened for it every time he heard the train whistle. Every night around midnight the train would come by.
Then he heard the screams. He heard how fearful Jason was at the end of it.

Calvin knew he was living in his own hell.

The track had been closed for years. Jason was gone and he wasn't coming back.

Calvin punished himself for years and he would continue to live in his parent's home. He would continue to listen to the whistle of the train and his brother's painful scream of that night long ago.

No punishment was greater than the punishment he gave himself.

It would be where he stayed until his final breath.

If he had been home Jason would be with him. That he knew as he felt the silent tears rolling down his face.

The End

Description

He heard an agonizing cry as he continued to walk the dirt road.
"A screech owl. You've heard it a hundred times before." He whispered to himself as he jumped, and his mind went wild.
He should've continued walking, he should've just kept going, but his feet stopped him.
He could see the house the porch light was left on for him.
Dillion could see his mother, she was doing the dishes and looking out the window. She was waiting for him, but she couldn't see him.
His feet had moved him to the side of the dirt road.
He could see her, he took a deep breath and let it out. Knowing she was waiting for him should've kept him walking.
It didn't.
"Help me, please, won't you help me?" The voice was of a little girl.
He had remembered back when he was little.
There she appeared!
In a white dress, a white ring surrounding her. She was glowing.
"Cassandra?" He asked, shocked when she smiled and nodded her head at him.
Why was she smiling though?
He remembered the tragic accident.
She was riding her bike up the dirt road. She was going to fast, and the busy road met the dirt road. That was it, in a blink of an eye she was gone.

They Always Come Back

That's what Dillion's friends had told him one night before he headed home. The dead. They always came back. The ones that hadn't crossed over to the other side.

Dillion thought about it as he walked the dirt road by himself. He tried to get the thoughts out of his head. Tried to make his feet walk a little faster.

He was already late; he didn't want to be any later and get into trouble.

In the brush that led out to a large field he heard rustling around.

His heartbeat quickened.

"Damn them." He muttered under his breath.

Though he would never cuss in front of his mother; he wished that he was home already. His friends had teased him.

They knew he believed in spirits. That he believed the dead could come back.

He heard an agonizing cry as he continued to walk the dirt road.

"A screech owl. You've heard it a hundred times before." He whispered to himself as he jumped, and his mind went wild.

He should've continued walking, he should've just kept going, but his feet stopped him.

He could see the house; the porch light was left on for him.

Dillion could see his mother, she was doing the dishes and looking out the window. She was waiting for him, but she couldn't see him.

His feet had moved him to the side of the dirt road.
He could see her, he took a deep breath and let it out.
Knowing she was waiting for him should've kept him walking.
It didn't.
"Help me, please, won't you help me?" The voice was of a little girl.
He had remembered back when he was little.
There she appeared!
In a white dress, a white ring surrounding her. She was glowing.
"Cassandra?" He asked, shocked when she smiled and nodded her head at him.
Why was she smiling though?
He remembered the tragic accident.
She was riding her bike up the dirt road. She was going too fast, and the busy road met the dirt road.
That was it, in a blink of an eye she was gone.
"Help me, please, won't you help me?" She asked him again.
She reached out and took his wrist.
Her hand was ice cold and he tried to pull away, but he couldn't.
A force so strong was making him go into the fields.
Looking over his shoulder he couldn't see his house anymore.
He couldn't see his mother who looked worried the last time he'd seen her looking up from the dishes that she was washing.
"I need to go home." He cleared his throat.
"I need to go home too." She giggled leading him further and further into the field.

Dillion knew about the accident. He hadn't seen it. No one had. Only her and the driver.

"He did it on purpose." She whispered.

"Did what?" Dillion was confused.

"He murdered me." Cassandra answered as if it was a simple answer to a simple question.

That's when Dillion saw the rundown shack. It was as if it had appeared out of nowhere.

Cassandra's father had been poor. He couldn't have her sleeping on the ground. He made a shack just for the two of them. Laid the flooring and put up the tin roof. They had lived like that when she was a little girl.

"Daddy." She peered through the window.

Dillion looked through the window too.

He didn't see anything at first. Then in the corner of the room he could see what looked like an old man.

"He hit me. He saw me and he hit me with his truck." Her voice was angry now.

Dillion's mouth went dry.

"No one helped me. You wouldn't help me, why wouldn't you help me?" She began to cry as she let go of his hand.

Dillion knew what he saw looking in through the window.

It was as if it was a crumpled bag of bones.

He turned, and ran as fast as he could, going home to his mother. He didn't stop running until he reached the porch.

Dillion was sweating when he slammed the door and pressed his back against it.

"Dillion, do you know how late it is? It looks as if you've seen a ghost." His mother lectured him.

His mother's voice was the best sound he'd heard all night, but he knew what he had to do for Cassandra. He had to tell the story of how she died. It was no accident and maybe, just maybe if he told someone the story that she had told him she could move on. They came back because they were stuck. Sometimes it was because they didn't believe that they were dead.

Dillion laid in bed that night staring up at the ceiling. He knew how he would help her. She let go of him for a reason. He had a purpose. To help her just like she wanted.

"I will help you Cassandra. I will set the story straight." He whispered.

Dillion got no sleep that night. He continued to hear her giggling and playing, riding her bike faster and faster towards the busy road.

The End.

Description

Jayden had gone to bed early he couldn't watch his mother go insane any longer. He didn't even know what to say to her.
How could she be smiling and laughing, humming and singing with family dying? It wasn't right.
He tried to think of anything that would make sense to him. None did.
Just as he was falling asleep, he heard his mother coming up the stairs. He heard her come into the room and bring the blankets up closer to him.
"Sleep child, everything will be alright." She whispered, kissing him on the side of his head.
It was then that his eyes opened wide.
His mother's lips were cold against his skin.
Her hands were cold when she rubbed the top of his head just as she had done when he was a little boy.

The Curse.

Jayden knew that his family was cursed. It seemed left and right people were dying. He began to wonder when he would.

Jayden was only sixteen when one by one his family was dying. He couldn't understand why they were happy, living in the house together. They'd lived there exactly one month when his mother got the call that his aunt had died. A week later his uncle. Then on the road, the trucker that his mother had grown to love died in a freak accident on the way home.

Jayden watched as his mother walked around the house as if nothing had happened. Strange to say the least.

He watched as she cleaned, humming, and sometimes even laughing. He knew that people grieved in different ways.

It wasn't until that night he understood it all.

Jayden had gone to bed early; he couldn't watch his mother go insane any longer. He didn't even know what to say to her.

How could she be smiling and laughing, humming and singing with family dying? It wasn't right.

He tried to think of anything that would make sense to him. None did.

Just as he was falling asleep, he heard his mother coming up the stairs. He heard her come into the room and bring the blankets up closer to him.

"Sleep child, everything will be alright." She whispered, kissing him on the side of his head.

It was then that his eyes opened wide.

His mother's lips were cold against his skin.
Her hands were cold when she rubbed the top of his head just as she had done when he was a little boy.
He waited until she left his room.
He slowly got out of bed and went to his bedroom door.
His mother was saying something. He wasn't sure what it was. She was talking so fast and so low that it sounded like she was telling someone a secret.
He crept out of the bedroom and down the hall to her room.
The door was open just a crack.
He peeked in through it and saw that she was in a black dress. A veil covering her face.
"We must never forget the ones who do wrong. We shall never forget the pain that they must suffer." Her back was to him.
He could see that there was a bowl in front of her. She was putting things inside of it, mixing it together.
"I call upon you now. I call upon the curse that has deemed me to hell!" She shouted out, raising her hands and throwing her head back to look at the ceiling.
"Whatever is done onto them is done unto you." The dark voice called back.
Smoke was coming from the bowl.
"I don't care." She was calm again, she giggled.
Jayden felt his heart racing; his hands were clammy and he felt the sweat slowly sliding down his forehead.
"Who is it that you want removed from this earth?" The smoke continued to rise and spread across the ceiling.

"Tommy down the street. He's promised to marry me; however, he's lying. His wife is with child. We've just found this out." She explained.

"For one that you take away, another is taken from you." The smoke warned her, letting her know the consequence of what she wanted done.

She only nodded her head though, this time she didn't speak a word.

Jayden rushed back to his room, slammed the door and covered up quickly.

His own mother was the one! She brought a curse onto the family! Each time she wanted something done it came back to her!

It wasn't until early afternoon that she went to Jayden's room. When she opened the door, he wasn't there.

"Jayden!" She shouted for him, her heart racing this time, her eyes wide.

She called for Jayden again and again.

He was nowhere to be found in the house. She ran outside and shouted his name repeatedly with neighbors surrounding Tommy's house.

She stood there; he was gone she knew this.

That's what he got for lying to her. Telling her that he would come to her, that if she got rid of the trucker, he would marry her, and they would be together forever.

"For everyone you take one is taken from you." The smoke showed up behind her.

She didn't have to ask what it meant.

She knew where Jayden was.

He was to never return to her. Never would see him again.

That's when the tears began to fall.
She went into the house, locking it behind her.
Some say she died inside; others say that she moved away.
Maybe she disappeared into thin air like Jayden, but no one could really tell what had happened to her.

The End

Description

The further he went off the trail the more his heart rate picked up. He didn't even know why he was nervous.
It wasn't as if his father had told him what was out there. Why he couldn't go off the trail. There had been no explanation if there had been, he hadn't paid any attention to it.
He stopped when he could no longer see the trail. Staring up into the dark sky. The stars shining and glimmering as they always did. Only more so now that he was deep in the woods.
He hadn't seen it until it was standing above him.
A shadow like thing was hovering above him. He could see the hands reaching down for him. Felt it grab him around his throat.
It wasn't until he was flat on his back that he realized what it was.

Shadow

Jake didn't have any friends, not really. He had a brother who tagged along wherever he went; and tonight, he was glad that his little brother had gotten into trouble for not cleaning his room; it meant that Jake could do whatever he wanted, he could go wherever he wanted.

He went out back of their house, going down trails that he hadn't been down in years. Now that he was older his parents didn't have to tell him to stay away from the woods. They didn't know that he was walking through the trails though.

If they had, they would've stopped him.

He never knew why his mother was so worried. Why she had such fear in her eyes when he was younger. It wasn't the first time that he had walked the trails as he got older. He walked them and nothing ever happened to him.

Then again, he had never strayed from the trails.

He remembered when he hit thirteen, his father told him he would be fine. That it would be their little secret.

His father told him to always stick to the trails so that he wouldn't lose his way back home. Jake thought it was funny now.

Laughing and shaking his head.

He laughed at himself.

At nineteen he was still listening to his father.

"Not tonight." He whispered to himself, looking over his shoulder and seeing the back of the house.

Tonight, he would prove to his father that there was nothing to worry about. He would come home safe and everything would be alright. He would call to his father and show him that he was still safe.

Jake felt as if he was doing something wrong when he stepped off the trail. He felt the dried leaves crunching under his shoes.

It was fall, his favorite season of all if someone were to ask him.

The further he went off the trail the more his heart rate picked up. He didn't even know why he was nervous.

It wasn't as if his father had told him what was out there. Why he couldn't go off the trail. There had been no explanation, if there had been, he hadn't paid any attention to it.

He stopped when he could no longer see the trail. Staring up into the dark sky. The stars shining and glimmering as they always did. Only more so now that he was deep in the woods.

He hadn't seen it until it was standing above him.

A shadow, like the thing was hovering above him. He could see the hands reaching down for him. Felt it grab him around his throat.

It wasn't until he was flat on his back that he realized what it was.

It was his own shadow!

He found it hard to breathe as he struggled with the shadow. The force it held, the way it gripped his throat tighter and tighter.

Jake couldn't believe what he was seeing. He couldn't believe that his own shadow was strangling

him!
Jake tried to cry out for help, no words came out.
Blinking faster and faster he watched as the stars began to disappear, the moon was full and high in the sky.
No one would find him. If he didn't return home his father would know, he would know that he had gone off the trail.
It had been their little secret that his father allowed him to go into the woods only as long as he stayed on the trail.
He had disobeyed the rule.
The shadow let out a loud cry, a screeching noise that hurt his ears so bad that he begged for it to stop in his own mind.
His brain screaming to make the noise stop.

Jake's father was sitting on the porch when he heard the screech that he had heard so long ago. He raced into the woods, staying on the trail as he was once told by his own father the night his brother went missing.
"Jake!" He shouted, calling his name again and again. The screech was so loud he had to cover his own ears. It was then he realized that Jake wasn't going to come home. Just like his own big brother hadn't come home.
Another one lost to the shadow.
Jake's father hit his knees and pounded the trail.
"Why? Why didn't you listen to me!?" He shouted again and again until he couldn't shout anymore.
The tears spilled out of his eyes and down his cheeks to wet the trail that Jake should've stayed on.

The End

Printed in Great Britain
by Amazon